WHIZZERS

WHIZZERS

A NOVEL

MICHAEL J. SAHNO

Published by:
SAHNO PUBLISHING
P.O. Box 46506
Tampa, FL 33646

First Edition
Printed in the United States of America

ISBN 978-1-944173-10-4 (paperback)
ISBN 978-944173-11-1 (ebook)

Publisher's Cataloging-In-Publication Data
(Prepared by The Donohue Group, Inc.)

Names: Sahno, Michael J., author.
Title: Whizzers / Michael J. Sahno.
Description: First edition. | Tampa, FL : Sahno Publishing, [2019]
Identifiers: ISBN 9781944173104 | ISBN 9781944173111 (ebook)
Subjects: LCSH: Recovering alcoholics--Fiction. | Nephews--Fiction. |
    Time travel--Fiction. | Consolation--Fiction.
Classification: LCC PS3619.A46 W45 2019 (print) | LCC PS3619.A46 (ebook) |
    DDC 813/.6--dc23

For Sunny,
The love of my life.

PREAMBLE

SOMETIMES YOU SEE ONE OUT OF THE CORNER OF YOUR EYE, BUT WHEN YOU LOOK IT'S ALWAYS GONE. Always. It may look like a bird or cat or insect, but only in terms of the motion, the velocity. You never actually see the shape. Some people dismiss these things as imagination, some as the ghost of an old pet: Pete the Bird, Truffles the Cat. No one ever considers them in terms of phenomena. Ophthalmologists even have a name for the condition that supposedly produces them: *dysoculogia*, literally, "abnormal or impaired vision."

Of course you want to know what they are, so why make you wait? The whizzers—so named because they "whiz" by you—are shadows. Not ordinary shadows, but soul shadows.

Let me explain.

Suspend your disbelief for a moment, if need be, and imagine you have a soul. Like someone told you when you were a kid. You probably believed it, not because they told you, but because in some way you felt it was true. You know you have a brain, and you've never seen it, right? Probably not.

But even if you've seen your brain, you've never seen your soul. So how would you know what it looks like?

The Far East provides some guidance here. For centuries, Eastern religions have maintained that the soul is a single point of brilliant light located between the eyebrows: the Third Eye. Consciousness delivers itself completely to this light during near-death experiences when people travel down the tunnel toward it. But what most people don't know is that when a person dies, the soul leaves the body in a form not of light, but of a cloud, or mist. One may see paintings or even movies that attempt to show this. Humans rarely have any awareness of the cloud, but animals do. They sense the shift in consciousness. It's why dogs howl when someone dies. They not only sense the change, they may even see it, and they mourn immediately. Most of us, though, will never see these clouds.

Still, like regular clouds in the sky, these soul-clouds cast shadows. And these shadows are the whizzers.

Unlike regular clouds, soul-clouds require no sunlight to cast their shadows. In fact, they work on the opposite principal: they're invisible on a sunny day. Only at night, or when it's cloudy and dreary, will you see one. And even then, only when you're in the right—or, you might more accurately say, the wrong—frame of mind.

How did I find all this out?

It all started like this....

ONE

THEY SIT OUTSIDE A MYSTERIOUS-LOOKING ROOM, PATIENTLY WAITING THEIR TURN: THEOCRITUS, JESUS, NIETZSCHE.... SEVERAL OTHERS WHO HAVE GIVEN ONLY THEIR FIRST NAMES UPON THEIR ARRIVAL. The lesser lights—Thomas Moore, Douglas Koeter, John Harkin—sit on the periphery, showing each other ancient dulcimers and lutes, playing with elaborate instruments, astrolabes and gyroscopes. When their names are called, they stand, looking serious and uncertain, as if they are being summoned to a judicial proceeding of mortal gravity.

Of course, I don't recognize them all. When you see a celebrity, you don't always realize who it is you're seeing. Especially when they've been dead for a couple hundred, or a couple thousand, years.

I've arrived here myself by way of what I thought was a dream, but actually turned out to be an out-of-body experience. I'd stayed the night at my cousins' house, sleeping in the bedroom of little David, the six-year-old, who camped out on his parents' floor so I could have his bed. I was plagued by vivid dreams throughout the night. Each successive dream grew stronger and more bizarre until, yielding to their influence, I realized I was not dreaming of ancient Mesopotamia at all, I was actually here. A hard experience to reconcile with a scientific mind. Still, the arrival of little David himself only confirmed my conviction.

David and I enter the lobby where the others wait. Right away I know something special is happening. I do not recognize most of the luminaries at first, either because I'm not familiar with them, or because they look different from the paintings I've seen. Jesus, for example, isn't nearly as effeminate-looking as in all those paintings. In fact, he's a little scruffy, and his skin is a hell of a lot darker than any of the famous Renaissance paintings that depict him. The first person I actually recognize is the poet Rabindranath Tagore, who looks exactly like the photograph I saw of him in an exhibition by the great photographer E.O. Hoppé. If I hadn't known him right away, I'd have wondered if he might be Socrates.

He is playing chess with a woman whom I'll later learn is Virginia Woolf, but I do not recognize her. I am only interested in him. I introduce myself and begin to introduce him to David.

"David and I know each other well," says Tagore. "He is one of the few among the living who has already advanced to the level of player."

I look at David and he smiles at my confusion. "Don't worry, Cousin Mike," he says. "I'll explain it all in a minute."

But no explanation will be forthcoming. At that moment the door to the mysterious room opens and a man in a long gold robe steps out to address the group.

"Will everyone else whose last names start with the letters A through M please step into the antechamber?"

"That's us," David says, and takes my hand. "See you later," he says to Tagore. We pass a man who grumbles, "It figures…they couldn't make it A through N," and David grins up at me again. "That's Nietzsche," he says. "You ever read him?"

"What!? Nietzsche?" I crane my head back around, but David leads me on. "Sure I've read him, but—"

"Yeah, he's always complaining about something. He's kind of a crank. I don't know how he ever got to be a player. M'Extezuh, the wizard who taught me, says he thinks God just wanted to make it up to Nietzsche for the whole mental breakdown thing."

My brain reels, but there's no time to think about it. The presentation has begun.

"Honored ladies and gentlemen, distinguished players … and guests—" the man in the gold robe nods in my direction "—it's time once again for our annual housecleaning." Everyone groans. "Now, I know you've all been looking forward to this about as much as you looked forward to going to the dentist in your previous incarnations—those of you who had dentists—but this year is going to be a little different."

A man in a black tuxedo motions to him, raising a finger. "Can we do some real ghost-type stuff this year? You know, clank some chains, make weird noises and whatnot?"

Several of the others laugh.

"No, Mr. Houdini, I'm afraid we'll have to rein in our predilections toward tomfoolery again this year. The main thing that's going to be different this year is each of you is going to have the opportunity to revisit your old home in the form of a whizzer."

A chorus of boos and groans rises.

"What's different about that?" a woman says. "We do that every year."

"But only in the present moment," says the golden man, smiling. "Not in your century of origin."

"Wait a minute," says another. "You're talking about time travel?"

"Not only am I talking about time travel. I'm talking about travel to *your* original time. Say you dropped your bodily form in AD 237. And you have always wanted to go back and comfort your grieving wife or husband or child. Or an ex-girlfriend, for that matter. But you couldn't do it, because it's generally forbidden, and you had work to do. Well, as players, you've all done an outstanding job, and now one of your rewards is the opportunity to go back to your time of origin, bring tremendous comfort, anonymously, to whomever you wish, and then—only after you've brought love and peace and serenity to your heart's content—only then will you have to do any housecleaning."

Houdini raises his hand. "Do we have to visit the people on Death Row again if we don't want to? I hate going there. It's *depressing*. Their stupid despair is almost contagious…I mean, I know they don't know how good life after death is going be, but still."

The golden man smiles. "Only the most advanced players need visit there: Jesus—" he nods toward the scruffy guy "—Mother Teresa…maybe Lao Tzu, if he promises to behave himself." Everyone laughs. "But no, only the most advanced players."

We walk back outside after the meeting into bright sunlight, and I turn to David. "How is it you're involved in all this? Tagore said you're one of the few among the living who's already advanced to the level of player. Why? What's it all about?"

He smiles. "You know what, Cousin Mike? You're about to find out."

And without another word he takes me by the hand and leads me past Nietzsche and Lao Tzu into the outskirts of the city, where poor people on park benches sit and nod to themselves, oblivious to everything around them. We pass a house of brick and stone near a field of purple flowers. We are no longer in the city. The road turns to dirt, and we pass old huts of bamboo and stone, open structures with places where windows should be, but are not.

"Where are we going?"

David looks ahead, expressionless. "We're going to see the Coordinator."

"The Coordinator."

"The man in the gold robe who was talking to all of us in the meeting."

"But isn't he still back there?"

David smiles now, and looks up at me. "By the time we get there, he'll already be where we're going."

"He can do that, huh?"

"He can do that."

I'm game. "So how come we can't?"

"We're still among the living."

"And him?"

The smile disappears, but he only looks reflective. "Dead for centuries," he says.

"And he's going to do what? Give us some special task? Tell you what you should do as a part-time whizzer?"

"It depends. He might have me do something different than the others. I really don't know."

"How do you know you're supposed to go meet him?"

"He told me."

"Before the meeting?"

"During it."

I arch an eyebrow. "He thought it, and you heard him."

He smiles up at me again. "You got it."

We walk on in silence. My six-year-old cousin travels through time and plays mental telepathy games with some sort of angel. He hangs out with Nietzsche and Jesus.

It's insane.

He and I are still among the living, but we are privileged enough to commune with the dead. And, of course, to go wandering back among the dead when they were not yet dead. When they were still opening mail, eating dinner, making love. When they needed comfort from the Great Beyond.

I feel as if someone has taken an oxygen tank and filled me up with fresh, cold air. I feel as if I am walking on air. I feel like Joe Frazier and Rudolph Valentino and Jesus of Nazareth rolled into one. I feel high as hell.

I feel like I did the first time I took a drink of alcohol.

And as David walks on silently, I begin to wonder what exactly this might be that I'm walking into, and what I want it to be. My exhilaration borders on terror.

I'm an alcoholic. I've been sober over twenty years, and those years have been the best of my life. I got sober the modern way. No pledges, no religious fanaticism. Just didn't drink and went to meetings and took their suggestions. But all my old heroes—and a good number of the new ones—were drunks or drug addicts. I think of the writers and artists and musicians I've always admired, and what I'd want to say to them if I could meet them. Almost without exception they overindulged. Faulkner. Fitzgerald. Hemingway. My musical heroes, too: Jimi Hendrix, Janis Joplin, Syd Barrett. And that great sixties protest singer, Phil Ochs. More names spring to mind. Thomas Wolfe. Dylan Thomas.

Billie Holiday.

Dear God, I think. What would I say to them? What *could* I say?

As if in answer, David breaks the silence.

"I guess we'll have to see who we meet and make them feel better if we can."

I realize this is an answer, and I turn to him again.

"You read my mind."

He smiles. "It wasn't hard to do."

"Did you hear me thinking, 'How the hell does a six-year-old know all this stuff?'"

A laugh. "That was about half an hour ago."

I laugh with him. "So how the hell *does* a six-year-old know all this stuff?"

He looks serious again and brushes back a lock of hair. "Remember when you were six?"

"No. I mean, I know I was a little precocious too. I remember wanting to be a paleontologist when I was eight. But six is harder to remember."

"You fractured your skull in a sledding accident."

I stop a moment and he pulls up alongside me. "You're right. That was one of the worst things that ever happened to me. I could have died."

"You could have, but you didn't. Remember how you felt when you woke up from the anesthesia?"

We continue walking. "Not really. Hell, a minute ago, I couldn't even remember the year. You want me to remember a specific day?"

"Think about it. The way that hospital smelled. And the *Peanuts* cartoon books on your bed. Remember that cute nurse?"

It all rushes back. "Good God, yes, even at six. She was like an angel to me. The kindest face, the voice…."

"She was twenty-one. Her name was Lynn. Picture the name tag."

Still walking, I close my eyes. "You're right. I can see it. And now I remember. I remember how I felt when I woke up. Before I saw the reflection in the mirror. Before I discovered they'd shaved my head clean. I was so pissed at that doctor."

"How did you feel? Before you saw yourself in the mirror."

"Oh, it was wonderful. Peaceful, beautiful. I felt like my life was beginning again. I remember looking out the window, sunlight pouring down through a cloudy sky…."

"That was a whizzer."

"What?" I break my stride again, open my eyes.

"A whizzer did that. Gave you that feeling. It helped ease the pain from coming off the anesthesia. And it prepared you for the shock of seeing yourself with no hair."

"That's unbelievable. I mean, I believe you, but—"

"Do you know the other time you were comforted by a whizzer?"

"Not at all."

He looks sidelong at me. "After you got sober."

Again I break stride, but continue on almost an instant later. "Really," I say. This is something I'm not prepared for. Not that anything could have prepared me for the rest. But David and I have never talked for even a moment about recovery. He's never seen me drunk, but I've never mentioned my alcoholism, either. I wonder what else he knows.

"Really," he says.

"You know pretty much everything about me, little man. Or so it seems."

He smiles again, pure acceptance. "Oh, not everything. I know about that girl in Binghamton, though. Deena?"

I blush to the roots of my hair, but when he starts to laugh, I can't help laughing too. "We won't even go there," I say.

"No, we won't."

"Do me a favor and don't tell your parents about that one, okay?"

"I won't tell my parents about any of this. Ever. They're on a different path than you or me."

"You mean *I* can't tell them about any of this either."

"By the time we're done, you won't want to. Trust me."

"I don't think I have much choice there. I have to trust you. But why do you know so much about me?"

"I know that kind of stuff about a lot of people. In some cases it helps, in others it doesn't. Help them *or* me. In your case, it might help you for me to know. I mean, at least if I know some of your blind spots, I may be able to help us avoid trouble later on. If it should come to that."

"Trouble?"

He smiles yet again. "I don't plan on having any. But there's no guarantee this will be easy."

That rocks me almost as much as "after you got sober."

"What do you mean?"

"We're not in what you call the physical world right now," he says. "It may look like it, and feel like it, but it's more than just the world you're used to experiencing. Can you understand that?"

"In theory. But what's different?"

"The possibilities."

"Bear with me here. What exactly are we talking about?"

"Let me put it this way. You've read a lot, right?"

"Sure."

"You've read Castaneda, right?"

"Yeah, I have."

"In some of those books, things happened that the ordinary person would never experience. Would never even believe in as possible events."

"Okay. I'm with you."

"That may be the case here. We may go off on our little mission and have an interesting time, with nothing all that unusual happening. Or it may get a little hectic."

"I don't like the way that sounds."

"I wouldn't expect you to. You know about a creature called the Dweller on the Threshold?"

"It sounds familiar."

"You know about it. Think back to all those Alan Watts lectures you used to tape off the radio."

"About Zen?"

"And about a whole bunch of other stuff. The Dweller on the Threshold is like fear made into substance: a monster, a big bug, a snake…whatever you're really afraid of, it takes on that form."

"I remember that concept now."

"And the only way to conquer it is to walk right at it. Maybe even right into it."

"You're telling me I'm going to fight Godzilla."

"No. But if he shows up, don't expect him to be your pal. Just remember he's not real. Don't lose your sense. Okay?"

I shake my head. "This sounds like something I should be telling you."

"I know. But I'm serious about this. I've seen it. My own version. And I didn't like it."

I pause, a chill seizing my spine. "What did it look like to you?"

He shakes his head. "I don't like to talk about it."

"Okay, but what are we talking about here? Is it fear made into substance, or could it do some real damage? I mean, if it's only some kind of bogeyman…."

"It could be anything," he says.

I notice the landscape has begun to shift. The trees are even sparser here than back in town, but it's not only that. Desert plains open out beyond us, and I notice only one place we could be heading: a gracefully curving hill in the distance that looks as though it can't possibly be inhabited by anything human, animal or vegetable. It's nothing but sand.

"That's where the man in the golden robe is waiting?"

He nods. "That's it. If we can make it to that spot with no trouble, our trip will be pretty much a fun time. We'll see."

"What do you mean, '*if* we can make it…?'"

"Like I said, the Dweller on the Threshold—"

Without warning, the whole landscape suddenly shifts wildly. Cacti appear out of nowhere, and the sun blazes above us so much brighter than a moment before, it's like a light being cranked to maximum wattage. We halt.

"What happened—?" I start to ask, but he says, "Wait." And then I see it. The Dweller.

It comes out of the sky like a living spaceship: a huge thing, brown and bristly, with wings like giant blades whirring. The vibration shakes the air, and sand flies into my eyes as it blows down across the desert right at us.

"Oh my God."

"Hold on," says David. "Just hold on and don't move."

I close my eyes. "What the hell is it?" But I get no response. I feel the breath of this thing on me, a slow blast of putrid air across the dry desert sand. Part of me expects it to eat me, but somehow I also know it can't be real. It can't. But what is it?

I open my eyes a crack, squinting to keep sand from blowing into them. I take a good look at it, as good as can be expected through quivering eyelashes.

It looks like a monstrous cockroach.

My mind leaps back inexorably to the boarding house I lived in on Arch Street. Three weeks sober, not a pot to piss in. Cracked walls, roaches on the ceiling. A catastrophic acid flashback, purple and orange and scarlet roaches scattering across the ceiling like grains of sand blowing across this desert floor. The fear of disease and death and insanity hammering in my chest. Those cockroaches weren't real. Most of them, anyway.

I open my eyes. I stride forward, toward the dreadful apparition, all anger and adrenaline, its hot breath like garbage in my face.

It vanishes.

I sink to my knees in the sand, hands over my face. I realize for the first time my body is drenched in sweat.

"Great job, Cuz," David says. "You did it."

"What? What did I do? And where the hell did *you* go?"

"I was right here. You just couldn't see me. As for what you did, you faced it. That's all you had to do. If you hadn't, I don't know what would have happened. I really don't."

"That was it. That was the Dweller."

"Apparently. You had a serious fear of roaches, huh?"

"I did."

We break down into laughter, and it feels like stitches tearing.

"Look," he says. I glance down to where he is pointing, and see a tiny cockroach scuttling away across the sand. Suddenly it all seems absurd. I'm panting so hard I can't laugh anymore, and I stand in the same spot for a long time, catching my breath. Then we begin to walk again toward the hill in the distance.

"How is it all this is going on?" I ask. "Are you really just my cousin David, or are you some kind of child guru, or what? I don't get it."

"I lead a dual life. Remember how you led a dual life when you were drinking?"

"Sure. Mr. Responsibility by day, Mr. Hyde by night."

"I do that too. Only, in a good way, not a bad way."

"What do you do?"

"Sometimes I just sleep through the night. Like normal kids. But mostly I go on these little excursions. I learn everything. But when I get up in the morning and go to school, I'm back to my typical self. The self you knew before. The one Mom and Dad know."

"Isn't that difficult for you? I mean, isn't it a lot of responsibility for a six-year-old?"

"When I go on my excursions, I'm like a dead person. My soul is at a different level. The souls of the dead, at that level, don't have responsibilities. But they get the chance to do good things. If they do them, great. If they don't, it's no big deal. No one thinks about failure."

"But do you *want* to do them?"

"Wouldn't you?"

"I don't know. Maybe. Yeah, I guess. Yeah."

We walk on. Eventually we close in on the place where the golden robed man lives, or will meet us, at any rate. It's over the crest of the gently curving hill we have reached, and when we cross over the top, we see it: a tiny golden castle in the middle of the desert, as unreal as anything I've seen all day.

"That's pretty unbelievable. That's where the guy in the golden robe is?"

"The Coordinator, right."

We walk slowly down. I don't know what else to say, and David is silent. When we reach the bottom of the hill, we walk across a long flat space of sand and scrub. David looks sidelong again at me, smiling.

"Don't be nervous, Cousin Mike. It's only an assignment. The worst part is already behind us."

I smile. "What makes you think I'm nervous?"

He arches an eyebrow, and it hits me again: he knows what I'm thinking and feeling before I'm even conscious of it myself.

"I guess you're right. A little gun-shy, maybe."

"Don't worry. We probably won't be going anywhere there are gunslingers. Not with the kind of people you want to meet."

I'm about to ask what he means, but we are outside the door already. The door knocker looks like some kind of brass gargoyle, and David can't quite reach it. I get the hint and lift the knocker.

The Coordinator himself answers. I don't know why, but I'd expected a butler or maid. He smiles his enigmatic smile, and ushers us in with a single word, "Welcome."

"Thank you," I say. "So you're the Coordinator. Tell me, what's this all about? Am I actually supposed to accompany David on some sort of 'whizzer' operation?"

"Please make yourselves comfortable," he says, indicating two soft-looking red chairs. "All will be explained to you in due course."

"What about all this business with dead people—no disrespect to present company intended—and the Dweller on the Threshold? Is that some sort of monstrous game cooked up to see if mere mortals can cut it?"

We sit down. "Not at all, Michael. The Dweller is as David explained him to you: the substance of all your fears made tangible. In your case, it resembled a gargantuan cockroach. Mine, on the other hand, bore a striking resemblance to my Aunt Valeria."

We laugh. "Okay. What about our little assignment here? David and I are going somewhere together, right?"

"That is correct. It would be presumptuous of you to expect to be advanced to the level of player immediately, although David's ascent was fairly rapid. Still, as Tagore told you earlier, David is one of the few among the living to have advanced to that level."

"Why am I not surprised you know Tagore told me that, even though you weren't around? Okay, then. What am I doing here?"

"You are to accompany David on his assignment, and your reward for doing so will be a chance to play the role of a whizzer. However, unlike the normal whizzer—who passes through people's lives invisibly and gives them some level of comfort—you will actually spend time with the people and, one must hope, be an even greater comfort to them.

"You won't change history, of course. There might be dire consequences for you if you tried. When you return, comfort or no comfort, it will be as if you never existed to them. The people you meet will have no recollection of having seen you at all."

"So, what's the point? If they forget about me right away, how much good could I have done?"

"The comforting itself is the gift, my friend. When you bring such comfort to another, you automatically get far more out of the experience than they ever could."

I look down. "I don't know if I've ever really bought that idea, but all right. And David?"

"I'm going with you," David answers. He looks up at the Coordinator for further confirmation. "Right?"

"Also correct," he says. "You'll serve as a guide, in much the same way you had a guide when you first went out. You remember."

"Sure," he says. He turns to me. "I had a really cool guide. He—"

"Ah-ah," the Coordinator says. "Don't forget the rules."

"Sorry." David turns back to me. "I have to wait until after our assignment is done before I can tell you anything about my first one."

"The enthusiasm of youth." The Coordinator smiles, and we all laugh. "And so," he says, "you will have to content yourself at first with following David, and then David will have to content himself with following you."

"Let me ask you something. What exactly *is* a player?"

He exchanges a glance with David, and it seems as if they both suppress a smile, although they look perfectly serious.

"I shall let David explain that one to you. For now, we must sleep. You have a long and strenuous journey ahead of you."

TWO

THE NEXT THING I KNOW, IT'S THE FOLLOWING MORN-
ING...OR SO I WOULD IMAGINE. I wake in a large, infinitely comfortable bed, and the Coordinator is nowhere
in sight. David is in another, smaller bed on the other side
of the room, lying in a pool of sunlight with an impish grin
on his face. He's dressed in long pants and a flannel shirt,
completely different from the previous day.

"Morning, Cuz," he says.

"What in the world happened?"

"You lost a little time there. I had to go back to being
Mr. Normal Kid for a while, and you needed some sleep.

Bet that was the fastest you've fallen asleep in a long time, huh?"

I groan and stretch, then get out of bed. "You know about my insomnia, too, eh?"

He laughs. "Yup. So, you ready to go?"

"Where are we going? Antarctica?"

He laughs again. "Nope. New York City."

"What?"

He laughs one more time, and when I blink, he's gone. It's as if the world has suddenly changed from a vibrant light to a dark cloud. I look around, and there he is again, but our surroundings have changed entirely. We're in some kind of warehouse, it seems, dismal and cold.

"How did you do that?"

"I didn't have to work too hard at it," he says. "I knew where we had to go, but it's basically your gig."

"Where is this place? You're telling me we just traveled through space to New York City?"

"Yup. We've got to get out of here, though, 'cause we have a show to catch."

"A show? God almighty." I notice my clothes are different now, too: dressed for winter. David puts on a jacket as we speak.

"Where are we going?"

"Can't tell you," he says. "Don't worry, you'll like it."

We hit the street, and right away I know we are in another time. The cars tell me early- to mid-sixties, though I can't be sure. Regardless, it's a massive jolt to my system.

"We're traveling in time, too? What are you taking me to see, a Broadway show?" I laugh, nervous now.

"Nope. We're going to Carnegie Hall. Come on, the show's already started, and it's sold out."

We hurry along the frozen street. "It's got to be January or February," I say. "This wind is terrible."

"Yup. And by the way, for the time being, we're invisible," he says. "But we're gonna be sneaking in through a back entrance, since we can't pass through the front doors."

"We can travel in time and space, but no ghost stuff, huh? Okay." I laugh, and he smiles. I can't believe a six-year-old is walking this fast.

We arrive at Carnegie Hall, and I'm struck by how easily we walk in the rear entrance…back before the days of high-tech security, I guess. The cold fades behind us, and suddenly I am standing still, and a chill runs up through me. From the warmth and darkness of backstage, I hear the voice and guitar of a man who will die by his own hand a mere ten years after this show. A contemporary of Bob Dylan's, a protest singer with a lilting tenor and a poet's heart. One of the most underrated songwriters of the twentieth century.

His name is Phil Ochs.

I look down at David, my mouth open, pure wonder surging up in my chest. He is studying me, curious but not too detached. I almost expect a smile.

"Let's get in there," he whispers. "There's some room up front, near the stage. There just aren't any seats."

"I don't believe it," I say.

But of course I do. Who else but Ochs? And here he is at the height of his powers, mesmerizing an audience with a song about lost love and lost youth, and about the passing of time, the inevitable cycles of life. A song called *Changes*.

We step into the auditorium, at a slight angle from the front of the stage. I can clearly see Phil in his jacket and tie, but I'm even more struck by the audience—so many of them transfixed, their young faces uplifted. I look to my left and see a young woman with long blonde hair, a tear rolling down her cheek. It seems as if the whole room is in that magical place where artist and audience meet, where the world melts away into a dream.

And then the song ends, the place explodes with applause, and the spell is broken. Ochs smiles and thanks them and carries on. I suddenly realize he's nervous—overcome, almost, with a bad case of stage fright—and the show is really not going too well for him. He hits bad notes occasionally, the guitar goes out of tune. His voice cracks a little. And though the audience is tolerant, even enthusiastic, I can guarantee the show will be harshly reviewed in the press, which will no doubt be devastating.

He is twenty-five years old.

He talks to the crowd in between songs, warming them up, getting them to laugh. He runs through songs about U.S. military operations in the Dominican Republic, songs about the heavy hand of fate. He is brilliant and funny and self-deprecating.

At the end of the show, he comes out to do an encore, a new song called *When I'm Gone*. It is as poignant and beautiful a song as any I've ever known, a statement about the life of the troubadour, his role as an artist and activist, and an eerie foreshadowing of his eventual tragic end. I listen with tears in my eyes, wondering why I've been given the privilege to travel back here to listen to this.

And then it's over. The applause fades out, and the audience begins to disperse through the brightened room. I turn to David and he grins.

"Come on," he says.

"Where are we going?" But there's no time to answer. We head outside and into the street, past the streaming crowd. Phil Ochs stands in the lobby, signing autographs, chatting with fans…as accessible as if he were new to the scene.

I see the concert poster outside the front door. It's Friday, January 7th, 1966.

"We can't stop and talk with them now. But we'll be with him and some friends later."

"You're serious. He's my whizzer prospect?"

"The first one, yeah. He drank a lot, huh? Like you used to?"

I look down at the boy beside me, hurrying along. "Yes, he did. He's going to kill himself in a few years, you know. These are the glory years for him. Before the real madness, before he self-destructs."

"I know."

We race down the street, passing taxis, neon lights, cars. A few snowflakes flutter past.

"David, in all seriousness, what the hell can I say to comfort this guy? He's going to end his life in total despair after a devastating depression. I can't prevent that. How can I possibly help him?"

"You can't perform a miracle. All you can do is say whatever's in your heart at the time."

I think about it. How *can* I help, knowing how the story will turn out in advance? I can't help wondering if this whole thing is pointless, some sort of cosmic joke that doesn't make any sense, and shouldn't. But David continues on, "It's okay to doubt your ability, but that doesn't mean your ability doesn't exist."

"What ability is that?"

"Your ability as a healer."

I think about that one. I don't have any ability as a healer, as far as I know.

"I'm not sure I know what you're talking about."

"Let me ask you a question. You meet a lot of alcoholics, right? You talk to them, try to help them?"

"Yeah, a few…I don't know if I'd say a *lot*."

"Some of them will still die drunk. You know that. What if you knew in advance someone you were talking to would still die drunk? Would you *not* talk to him?"

Christ, this kid has my fucking number. My eyes cloud up. "Of course," I say. "Of course I'd still talk to him." I have to pause, and I actually gasp back a sob, overwhelmed.

He smiles, and for the first time since the beginning of our trip, when he led me past Lao Tzu and Nietzsche and out of the city, he takes my hand. "Don't worry," he says. "Everything's going to be all right."

"I know," I say. "I know."

We hurry down the street. Cars fly past, and an occasional snowflake. We reach the destination, a bar called The Kettle of Fish. I look toward David again.

"We're going into a bar?"

"*You're* going into a bar," he says. "I'm too young. Don't worry, I'll be close by. And you'll know when it's time to leave."

"Jesus, a bar. I don't go into bars at all anymore," I say, more to myself than anyone else. Suddenly, I notice the people walking by me are staring at me, as if I were another one of those hapless souls wandering the streets, talking to themselves. And in that moment, it dawns on me: they can't see David, only me. They really do think I'm talking to myself.

Obviously, I'm no longer invisible, but David still is.

I look at him, and he nods and winks. Then he laughs silently and vanishes.

I face the door. I really don't much like the idea of a bar. Sure, I'm sober, but that's the whole point. I don't belong in there anymore.

Then I remember: do I have a legitimate reason to be there?

Yes, I do.

And do I want to get drunk?

No, I don't.

The bouncer at the door looks me up and down. "Can I see some ID?"

I smile, but inside I panic. I can't be handing him an ID card from the wrong century, for God's sake. But I reach into my pocket on faith and pull out my wallet. Sure enough, everything's been arranged. I even have a fake address in the Bronx.

He hands it back. "Here you go." I thank him and pocket it, giving it a quick glance. I look like myself in the picture, but with the wrong hair. It's styled for the times, a style I've never had in my life. I walk in and head straight for the bathroom to see for myself.

Once there, panic subsides as I study my reflection in the mirror. It is truly bizarre. I am myself, yet not myself. My hair is different, of course, but much more: not only are the clothes and the driver's license foreign to me, I even have a pair of glasses I've never seen before. I decide to check out the contents of the wallet.

Here is my license from the state of New York. Here is a New York City Public Library card. I pull out all kinds of stuff, unfamiliar but with my name, my signature—it's as though I've committed the identity theft of my own double and filled in his shoes for him. I study the money. Yes, even the currency is appropriately old, the dates on the bills showing they were printed in the late fifties and early sixties. Nothing left to chance.

I walk back out to the bar, feeling much more relaxed. The place is packed, dense with cigarette smoke. These are the old days, I remember, before all the laws against public smoking. The place reeks of tobacco, stale beer, and cologne.

The bartender looks at me with a brotherly expression. "What can I get ya?"

I order a coke, taking a quick sniff of it before I drink it, in case he thinks I meant a rum and coke. But nothing to worry about. Pure cola, syrupy sweet and highly carbonated. I lean back against the bar and survey my surroundings, enjoying the comfortable anonymity of a stranger in the big city.

After a few moments of letting my eyes settle where they will, I notice a room in the back with people sitting around tables covered with drinks and large ashtrays. The room is dark, but even from here I can tell this is where the local celebrities meet. It has that aura. A few of them are playing cards, and then I hear someone strumming a guitar.

Of course, I walk back.

Nobody pays me any attention, so I sit down. They're all young men, and I study their faces, wondering which of them are well-known. One of them looks like a young folksinger named Tom Paxton, but I'm not sure if it's him. Their hair is long for the times, though conservative by any standard since.

"Where's Dylan tonight?" one of them asks.

"I think he's back in the studio again, man. Ochs must be finishing up his big Carnegie Hall show right about now. He'll probably be here."

"You think he really sold it out, or what? I don't know how he could have done it."

"It's possible. The tickets were only two or three bucks, man. We could all fill the place for those prices."

"Shit, they would have *lost* money on the deal, then. You think that's what they did? For publicity?"

"That, and Phil always wanted to sell out Carnegie Hall."

They keep dealing the cards, talking and smoking, and the conversation quickly turns to other things. Vietnam, the fear of getting drafted. Splitting for Canada.

One of them, a young-looking guy with a handlebar mustache, turns to me. "Hey, man. You want to play some gin rummy? No money on it."

"Sure."

We exchange introductions. I don't recognize his name, but the people he introduces me to are familiar names from sixties' folk: Eric Andersen, Dave Van Ronk. And, as I suspected, young Tom Paxton.

"Hey, boys," we hear from outside the room, and in comes Phil, fresh from Carnegie Hall. He is still wearing his white shirt and black tie, looking more like he's on his way to church than entering a bar.

"Ochs," they say in unison, and everyone laughs. "Put that goddamn guitar down and get yourself some scotch."

Phil laughs and joins us, taking off his winter coat. "Where were you guys? I didn't see you in the front row."

"We all had gigs, too, man. We just got here. Nothing

big time like you, of course." They laugh again. "So how were things down at Fifty-Seventh Street and Seventh Avenue?"

"Not bad," he says, avoiding eye contact. "I guess I was a little nervous. My marvelous family came down." He takes a drink proffered from a pint of whiskey.

"Where are they now? You should have brought 'em here." Everyone laughs at this one.

Phil laughs, then catches my eye. "Who's this, the next Bobby Dylan?"

They laugh, and I introduce myself.

"I'm Phil," he says simply. "You're not with the FBI, are you?"

We all laugh. "Not even close," I say.

"I didn't think so. Not with that hair."

I laugh again, struck by the surreal nature of the scene.

"Most of these guys are famous musicians with big hit records, so we're in good company here," adds Phil. They all laugh again at the sarcasm. "Hey, you guys see today's papers?"

Phil pulls out a stack of newspapers from inside his guitar case: the *Times*, the *Post*, the *Tribune*. The conversation returns to Vietnam, and I keep my mouth shut. It would be too easy to say something about a future event. I think about the Vietnamese, the Cambodians, the Laotians, the indiscriminate slaughter of thousands thanks to Nixon and Kissinger and all the other war criminals in their employ. No, better he not know—he'll take it all too much to heart as it is.

An hour later I retreat to the bar for another coke. When I look up, I see Phil has followed me. He looks out the window, then back at me. "You know what America is?" he asks.

"An experiment gone awry?"

He looks at me hard, his dark eyes darker than before, as if the pupils had swallowed the irises whole. "America is two Mack trucks colliding on a superhighway because the drivers are on amphetamines."

I laugh. "It really is bedlam, isn't it?"

"Yeah. Maybe I just need to get out of this town for a while. Breathe some fresh air." He looks back out to the street.

"You know what, though?" I say this, and when I look up, I see my little cousin David standing right outside the bar, smiling, nodding at me. I go on. "In spite of all that, and in spite of everything we've been talking about for the last hour, I've got to believe everything's really gonna be all right in the end." I put my hand on his shoulder for an instant, looking him dead in the eye as he looked at me a moment ago. "Seriously, man. You're gonna be okay."

He laughs, and I feel his shoulder relax before I remove my hand. "Maybe you're right," he says. "Who knows?"

The bartender hands us our drinks and says, "Mr. Ochs, you have a phone call."

"Thanks." He pulls the receiver over the bar. "Ochs here."

I look down again to where David is standing. He nods again, and I know it's time to go. For the first time that evening, I feel the weight of sadness. I want to rescue Phil Ochs somehow, drag him away and save him from his fate, from the suicide ten years hence. But it's time to go. I look at my watch, mouth *I gotta go*. He shakes my hand, talking a mile a minute on the phone as I head for the door.

THREE

DOWN THE DARK STREETS AGAIN, PAST SWIRLING SNOWFLAKES AND THE BRIGHT NEON LIGHTS OF THE CITY, WALKING FAST. Past newsstands, shining store windows with mannequins and Christmas lights. I still don't know what to say or how I should feel, but the turbulence in my chest keeps me quiet for a long, long time. David walks beside me quickly, silent as well.

"So why don't I feel better?" I finally ask.

"Because he's still going to kill himself."

I stop at the street corner, and David stops beside me. "Damn it, I *know*. Why? It doesn't seem fair that we couldn't at least do something for him."

"What could we possibly have done?"

"Hell, I don't know. We *can't* change the past, that's the whole problem."

"Remember your old Alan Watts lectures? Remember the Eastern concept of the universe as a play?"

"Sure. 'All the world's a stage and all the men and women merely players....'"

"You know, Phil Ochs saw his life as if it were a movie."

"Yeah? And?"

"And he chose the end of the movie. Not you."

We stand at the corner, silent. I tap my foot, holding myself against the cold. "Shit." I say nothing else for a while, blowing cold air into the night. "Tell me something. As bad as I feel right now, what could I possibly get out of this? I can't believe the tiny bit of comfort I was able to give that man for two seconds is going to do him or me any good in the long run."

"If you went back home and forgot all about it, you'd be right. But this is just the beginning. There has to be a cumulative effect."

"A cumulative effect of what? More misery all down the line?"

"No. More gratitude."

I'm stunned. "Gratitude? For what? My own situation?"

"You got it. That, and you'll no longer take yourself so damn seriously."

This cracks me up, and David laughs as well. "Geez, you know I take myself too seriously, eh?"

"Cuz, if there's one thing about you I know, it's that

you take yourself too seriously. That was a no-brainer."

I laugh again. "Only sometimes, you know. It used to be much worse."

"I know that, too." He laughs again, more like a kid than before. I suddenly remember his actual age.

"Oh, shut up." I reach over and muss his hair. "You little smartass. Jesus, a six-year-old guru."

He laughs again. "Not a guru, exactly, but I'm definitely well informed about a few things. Better than *you* ever were." And he laughs again, dancing away from me, acting his age for a change. I can't help smiling. He sticks his tongue out at me, and I laugh.

"Where are we going now? Someplace warm, I hope."

"As a matter of fact, we are going someplace warm. But first, you've got to rest again."

"You're kidding. We just woke up before we came here."

"I know, but this kind of travel takes it out of you. Trust me, you'll feel rested. Ready to go?"

"You're gonna do that number again, where the next thing I know it's morning, huh?"

He laughs. "Whenever you're ready."

"No time like the present, I guess." I smile and close my eyes.

FOUR

WHEN I AWAKE IT IS MORNING, AND WE ARE INDEED
IN A ROOM SIMILAR TO THE LAST ONE WE LEFT BEFORE
THE NEW YORK TRIP. I look around. David is asleep this
time, his face turned to the wall. I walk over and look down
at him, whispering, "You awake?"

No answer. His breathing is silent, his small form perfectly still. He looks like anything but a wise man. He is six
years old. He looks six years old.

I tiptoe around the room, glancing at the furniture, the
curtains. It is exactly the same as the room we left before,
I think, until I notice a small framed canvas I don't recall

seeing. I walk over to look at it more closely. The canvas is pure white except for six or seven dots of black paint in no apparent pattern. Some kind of abstract pointillism in black and white, I suppose. I don't get it. A six-year-old could do a better job, I think. I look over at David and smile. Much better.

As if my thought has reached him—and who knows, maybe it has—he turns and stretches. "All set?" he asks.

I laugh silently. "No 'Good morning, Cousin Mike?' No 'Morning, Cuz? How are ya?'"

He giggles. "I forgot you were here. I was dreamin' about this girl, Eugenie."

"Eugenie? Jesus Christ."

"No, no, not Jesus Christ. Just Eugenie."

I laugh out loud. "Good grief. You don't take after any strangers, do you?" I sit back down on the edge of the bed, my head in my hands. He laughs at me, and I shake my head.

"Don't worry, Mike. I haven't kissed her or anything. Remember, I'm only six."

I look up at him, grinning. "How old is *she*?"

He laughs drily. "She's six, too."

"Oh boy. She's six, too. That's great."

"So, you ready?"

"You said we were going someplace warm, right? We going back to Florida?"

"Close."

I look at him, still grinning. "Close?"

"Oxford, Mississippi."

FIVE

BEFORE I HAVE TIME TO SAY OXFORD, MISSISSIPPI? WE ARE THERE. We stand in a small grove of scrub pines, at the base of a long sloping hill that climbs into a forest. It's spring or summer, but cloudy and overcast, and our clothes have once again changed completely.

I pat my pockets instinctively for my wallet or keys. Nothing.

"This is Oxford, Mississippi," I say.

David nods.

"You're serious."

He nods again, then smiles up at me.

"*Faulkner?*"

The smile disappears, but he nods once more.

"My wallet is gone."

"Don't worry," he says. "You won't need it."

"What year is it?"

"I dunno. Nineteen-twenty something."

"You don't know? Then how are we supposed to communicate with anybody if we don't know what year it is? And no ID."

"It won't matter. You're not going to see anyone but him anyway."

"What?"

"Look." He points into the distance, and I see a young man at the end of the stand of pines, walking slowly. Hands in pockets, smoking a pipe, of all things.

"Good God. I don't know what's going on with this man. What the hell am I supposed to do?"

"You'll figure it out. Make small talk. Trust me, he'll be at least as interested in you as you are in him. He's a writer." He smiles.

I laugh. "He's a writer, all right." I pause, my hands suddenly cold. "All right, I'll see you later, I guess. Is that the deal? God knows I don't know what I'm doing."

"Don't worry, I'll be back." He laughs, and walks away, waving.

I walk slowly toward William Faulkner. My hands are too cold to shake hands with him. I don't want to make myself even more conspicuous by rubbing them together. It's not cold enough outside to do that. So I put my hands in my pockets, trying to look relaxed, like him.

He can see me from quite a distance. It's so quiet out

here, no one could miss me. Nothing but the wind in the pines between us.

I manage a casual wave from far away, like any stranger would give to acknowledge another's presence.

He nods, still not close enough to tell if I'm a neighbor or a total stranger.

I get close enough for a greeting.

"Morning."

He stares through a cloud of smoke, puffing the pipe. For a moment I do not think he is even going to speak. But then he blinks, removes the pipe from his mouth, and with a half-smile, he says, "Yep. It's morning, all right."

"Not a bad day for a walk," I say. "You live around here?" As if I didn't know.

He nods again, his black eyes flashing. "I live here," he says. "You're not from around here, though. That accent sounds like Connecticut or Rhode Island or something."

I laugh, and I can see him loosen up a little. "Good ear," I say. "I live in Florida, but I'm from Connecticut originally."

"What are you doin' here?"

"Just passing through," I say. We begin walking, side by side, along the edge of the forest. "My aunt used to live in Jackson, and I was on my way there…thought I'd take a break from the drive." I'm making this up, suddenly surprised how the fiction flows out so smoothly from me.

"Not a bad day for a drive," he says.

For a moment I wonder if this is an invitation to get off his property. But then I remember why I'm here. I must continue on, though he scarcely seems to need any sort of comforting at the moment.

"So, what do you do out here?" I ask. Again, as if I didn't know.

"Got a farm," he says. "Tough way to make a living, but it ain't all bad."

I try not to smile. "Quite a nice area, actually. How long have you lived here?"

"Most of my life. Been overseas a bit, but mostly here. How you like livin' in Florida?"

"I like it. I don't like the cold."

"Hotter'n hell all summer, though, isn't it? Like here."

"That's all right," I say. We come to a place where the path alongside the forest opens into a wide bottomland, with a dirt road winding east into more woods. We begin walking up the dirt road.

"Name's Faulkner," he says. "Bill Faulkner."

"I'm Mike."

"You know something?" he says, glancing over. I notice his eyes are bloodshot, surprised I hadn't noticed before.

"What's that?"

"This is a hell of a place to try to live. Hell of a place."

I nod, waiting to see if he expects a response.

He goes on. "See that house up there?"

I look to where he points: an old wooden house, probably a plantation mansion in its time. Now it is nearly fallen down, the portico rotting, no sign of human habitation.

"Looks abandoned," I say.

"Yep, might as well have been. That was the Compsons' place. Some family. Had a big imbecile kid they called Benjy and a daughter named Caddy and a couple other boys, Jason and Quentin...."

I know the story. I first read *The Sound and the Fury*

when I was eighteen, more than fifty years from the date we are walking through. He is talking about characters he's created, and now I know it is the late nineteen twenties, and he has probably just finished the book, or he's still deep under its spell. He is spinning a tall tale for me about these characters as if they really were people, as if they had lived in that rotting old house with its fallen beams and shattered windows.

"That Jason was the evilest son of a bitch you ever saw," he says. "Stole all the money his sister sent for his niece and all the while saved every last nickel he could from the store he was clerking in, too. He got his, though." He laughs. "Yep, he got his."

"What happened?"

"His niece stole all his money and took off, lickety-split. Just like that." He snaps his fingers and smiles—a shy, proud, devilish smile. "She didn't even know she was stealing her own money back from him."

I laugh, and he laughs, too. "What a family," I say.

He shakes his head as if in disbelief, staring hard into the house, through it, beyond it. "Yeah," he says. "What a family."

We stop, looking up at the house as if it were going to speak. It is only when we have stopped walking that I realize what I should have noticed when I noticed his bloodshot eyes: the dank odor of liquor coming out of his pores from the previous night's drinking. I glance at him again. Like Phil Ochs later in the century, he will never find sobriety either. He will carry the pain of the world on his shoulders, making it into art again and again, but never happy, never knowing any but a transitory contentment.

What can I possibly say? I think of the little bit I said to Phil, how insufficient it seemed, how little good it seemed to do even me. I imagine I must do more here, and try to think where to begin.

"What about the other people living there?" I ask. "I mean the servants you mentioned—Dilsey, Lucius, all of them—how did they endure it all?"

He pauses, nodding, still staring at the house. "They endured," he says at length. "They endured."

Another long silence as I recall how his lifelong empathy for the plight of southern blacks manifested itself in his work over and over.

Out of nowhere, I remember the words of the Coordinator: *When you are gone, comfort or no comfort, it will be as if you never existed. The people you meet will have no recollection of having ever seen you at all.*

I think about Phil Ochs, how hesitant I was to really tell him anything. Then it hits me like a cold blast through the humid Mississippi air: I can say whatever I want. It doesn't matter. It can only help and cannot harm…I just can't try to change the facts of history. And when I am gone, it will be as if I never existed.

I look at Faulkner. What would he say if I told him about Martin Luther King, the Freedom Riders, the whole civil rights movement? Even more pressing, what would he say if I told him I came from the future?

Then I think again: how much would anyone really care about the future of everyone else? Human nature would drive almost anyone to wanting to know about their own future first.

"Listen, Bill," I say. "I don't know how else to tell you this, so I'm just going to tell you. I wasn't born in this time period, and don't even know all that much about it. I was born in 1964, which is what…about thirty-five years from now?"

He looks at me, smiling. "Phil Stone put you up to this, right? That sumbitch is always trying to find someone to come tell me something crazy…."

"Nobody put me up to anything, Bill. I'm serious. I'm not an alien, and I'm not a lunatic from the Jefferson asylum. I know all about *The Sound and the Fury* because someday they'll be reading it in the schools, along with a lot of your other books. You're going to be big, Bill. Really big. But I can't promise you it'll be easy."

His face turns grey at the mention of the title of his book; almost as if he knows right then and there that I'm not bullshitting him.

"God damn," he says. "God damn." He takes a step back.

"Don't worry, I'm not a ghost or a dead man, either. I'm on a sort of assignment."

"From who? The fuckin' devil?"

I laugh. This isn't going quite as well as I'd hoped. Have I made a mistake?

"No. It's a long story. But I wanted to tell you you're going to be all right. I know you're worried nobody will buy the damn book, since they didn't buy *Flags in the Dust* yet, either, but they will. You really don't need me to tell you that."

"You're serious, aren't you?"

"Yeah, I am."

"You could have gotten that information about my books from one of the other people who knows me. You know that, don't you?"

"Yeah. But what stranger would bother to come up to you and start talking this shit…seriously. Do I look like someone playing a prank?"

He stares hard at me, the color returning to his face.

"You sure as hell don't. That's what scares me."

"Nothing to be afraid of, Bill. That's what I'm here to tell you. You wrote your guts into that book, didn't you? The way you told me about it now, you'd think you lived every moment of it yourself."

"I did write my guts into it. Yeah, I did."

"You should keep doing that. And you already know that, too, and you *will* keep doing it. That's all I'm here to tell you. Keep fighting the good fight."

"Why me? Why am I so special to get this…visitation?"

"No idea, Bill. Why am I so special that I get to make it? That's what I'd like to know. And I *don't* know. I really don't."

He laughs, and I see him loosen up a tiny bit again. "God damn."

"By the way," I say. "I'm a writer too. My name's Mike. Did I mention that before?" I shake his hand again, as if just introducing myself.

He laughs harder, sweat beading up on his brow. "Dunno. So, will I be reading your stuff when I'm an old man?"

"Sorry, but you'll be gone before I'm ever published. I appreciate your influence on me as a young man, though. Your books did a lot for me at a time in my life when things were very dark and painful in a lot of ways."

"That's good to know. Guess that's what we all want, isn't it? A receptive audience. Am I…am I gonna die young?"

"I can't really tell you anything like that…but I will say you'll live an incredibly full life and write some real masterpieces. Seriously."

He shakes his head again. "God damn."

"I wish I could do more for you. I really do. But all I can do is tell you you're going to be all right. You'll do what you came here to do. By the way, you won't remember meeting me or anything I've said now. Hopefully, it'll get into your blood somehow and help you keep going when things get rough. I don't know."

"Well, thanks. Shit, thanks a lot." He seizes my hand, and I can see by the look in his eyes what I've said has helped, at least for the moment…beyond that, I guess it's none of my business.

"You're welcome, Bill. Like I said, I wish I could do something more."

"You *sure* I won't remember any of this?"

"Pretty sure, yeah."

"What did you say your name was again?"

"Mike." I look away, and David is there. Giving me the nod again.

"Mike what?"

I look at Faulkner. He releases my hand and I smile.

"Let's just leave it at Mike," I say.

SIX

BOOM, I'M GONE. For a moment I imagine Faulkner's face, seeing me vanish before his eyes, but then I remember: I'm doing the job of a whizzer, and he won't recall a thing. I am insubstantial as a ghost.

I wake in the room again, the one with the painting on the wall, but this time it's just me; no David. I pace the room, looking for signs he's been there. Nothing. It occurs to me to wonder for the first time whether this is actually the same room each time, or just a similar-looking one. From the start I've assumed it's a bunch of similar rooms—like hotel rooms but decorated as if they were the combination of a young boy's room and a guest bedroom. The odd pointillist-style painting looks like it has a few more dots on it than last time I saw it, but that's surely my imagination.

I try the door. It's locked.

Now panic sets in. I don't like being locked in from the outside, not even when I know where I am. And I most definitely do not know where I am.

I go for the window, but it's also locked. Outside the window, it's dark. Nothing to see. Only an inky blackness, punctuated with neither stars nor moonlight.

I stare out into it for a long time, looking for clues—shapes of buildings, anything. It's like looking into the darkness of a sealed tomb. I wait for my night vision to make an adjustment that will yield something, but nothing happens.

I turn out the lights.

My heart is pounding. Still, I try to remain calm. I sit on the edge of the bed in a meditative posture: palms upraised, the backs of my hands lying loosely against the thighs. I close my eyes, and darkness gives way to a slow fading purple lightshow, the receding shapes I always see when I close my eyes. I watch them until my mind grows calmer, my breathing slows, my heartbeat returns to normal.

I need to focus on my thinking. Why the panic? Because I feel claustrophobic? Or because David isn't here? It's hard to believe I have come to rely on him so much, that in this situation it's almost like he's the parent and I'm the child. I don't know where I'm supposed to be going next or what I'm supposed to be doing.

I think about it. Why isn't he here, and what if he doesn't show at all? I could perish in this locked room in a matter of days. I looked around for food or a phone or an entrance to even a bathroom, but found nothing. In spite of feeling foolish about doing it, I speak his name tentatively into the darkness.

"David?"

I wait. Nothing happens, and the room is completely silent. No sound filters into it from outside. I decide it is less like a hotel room and more like a room in outer space.

Still, it makes no sense to panic. I know that much, even if I feel panicky inside. I suspect the best thing to do is try to relax and wait a while for David to materialize.

I turn the light back on and lie back on the bed, hands behind my head, trying to relax. I look at the ceiling and think. What should I do next? Probably nothing. Just wait.

The central air conditioning unit sighs to a halt, and I realize I've been hearing it all along without noticing it. We must certainly be in at least the late twentieth century, or a reasonable facsimile. So, okay. Where the hell is David? After the Ochs encounter, he was automatically there. I realize I've expected a certain pattern to exist even though it hadn't really established itself as such. It would be one thing if David appeared there with me after Ochs and Faulkner and then other people, but there have only been those two. I begin to think my expectation ridiculous.

Back to meditation, since I don't feel like I can sleep and there's nothing else to do here. I return to the seated posture on the edge of the bed, legs dangling to the floor.

It takes a long time to go out again, as if I were back to square one. After about twenty or thirty minutes, I am back to the fading purple forms phase. I'm reminded of a long meditation I went into once during a massage therapy session. I remember I watched the fading pattern until I wanted to possess it, to keep the moment and the feeling firmly there within my grasp. And as soon as I tried to control it, it slipped away like a fish in fast-moving water—gone, not to be glimpsed again. I enjoyed the rest of the session, and still felt relaxed, but I regretted trying to capture that elusive magic and thereby losing it.

This meditation becomes even better than that one was. Perhaps it is the open-endedness, the fact that I'm not working within a timeframe. David isn't here, and I don't know when to expect him. So I watch the purple fade and grow, ebbing and flowing, until at last it begins to resemble a kind of lake. Then it hits me: this is like looking at something I used to see with my eyes closed when I was a child. I would lie in bed at night and press with my fingers on my closed eyes, watching the riot of light and color it produced. I called these excursions "eye glace," and they were like a childhood precursor to psychedelics.

At the end of each of these little explorations, I would suddenly release the pressure and watch the colors fade and fade and fade, changing and swirling in fantastic shapes. And always, somewhere toward the end of the fade, there would be what I called the green lake: a shimmering, greenish-gold amorphous thing with an edge that looked like golden lace. It would morph again and again, fading and reappearing, and it mesmerized me. I didn't know if it signified something profound or if it was merely something I liked to see, but I always chased it. And during that meditation years later, when I tried to capture the elusive purple pattern, I had seen much the same thing, though without having pressed on my eyelids to create optical phantasmagoria.

I can't help but wonder now if it's somehow all connected, if there is a link among all these things…whizzers, purple patterns, the Third Eye. But I know I have to let go of all thought and follow the meditation wherever it takes me. Usually I don't think of words during moments like this. I simply let go of all thought, and the meditation happens the way it's supposed to happen. Somehow I find myself remembering lines of poetry written long ago in a place far from my own life and experience:

> *In Xanadu did Kubla Khan*
> *A stately pleasure dome decree:*
> *Where Alph, the sacred river, ran*
> *Through caverns measureless to man*
> *Down to a sunless sea…*

Coleridge, I think. That's Coleridge's *Kubla Khan*. What in God's name made me think of that? I'm surprised I remember that much of it so clearly, since I haven't read it or even thought about it since college. I can't imagine anything having to do with whizzers or the Third Eye would be connected to a poem written in 1797 by a man in an opium dream.

Even more strange is the way I suddenly feel. Before my visits to Ochs and Faulkner, I had a brief sensation like falling. Then, without warning, I was in the past. Now I have a similar sensation, though it seems to come slowly and lasts much, much longer. Almost as though I'm floating. It's a peaceful sensation completely in line with the meditation, but then I wonder: what if I'm time-traveling again, but alone? The thought scares me, and now the falling sensation speeds up and I open my eyes, feeling a little dizzy. I get up to turn on the lights.

No lights. I grope in the darkness along the wall, but find no switch. I am sure there was one earlier. I know I turned off a light before I started this meditation, because I turned it back on and then off again. But I can't see well enough in the dark to find even a lamp. My hands feel for objects on the nightstand. Maybe there is a flashlight, something.

I feel a candle, which I do not recall having seen before. I fumble for matches and find some. I light a match, and the room comes to life with a soft glow.

It is not the same room.

By the light of the candle, I look at my reflection in the mirror. I am not the same person. Every item of clothing I had on before is gone. My hair is in a style so foreign to me, I almost gasp in fright. I look as if I've stepped out of a painting by Watteau, all heavy coat and waistcoat, breeches, leggings. I look down: my shoes have buckles.

Buckles!

I say what anyone would say.

"Oh, shit."

My voice. It is hardly what I would call my own. I say it again, not only because of what I'm feeling, but also just to hear it.

"Oh, shit."

British. Dear God, it cannot have happened. I could no more survive in Coleridge's world than he could in mine.

I try the door again, unthinking, acting out of pure panic. It opens.

Outside, the night is black and cold, but not too cold. I can endure it in my heavy coat and waistcoat, though I am afraid to step beyond the threshold.

Then I think about that word, *threshold*. I remember the Dweller on the Threshold, my irrational fear, and it strikes me: aren't fears in general irrational? Surely I've come through all this without a scratch, and with David by my side I've felt confidence in the midst of extremely unnerving situations. That he doesn't appear to be here tonight shouldn't deter me from continuing on with my mission, whatever it may be.

Off I go into the night, looking back occasionally at what turns out to be a kind of small cottage. I wonder where I am, where I should be going. If I get lost, I have no idea how to get back to where I am now. But there is not a soul in sight to ask—only the moonlight to guide me. There was no moonlight before, only that foreboding blackness, and I wonder what's been orchestrated here. Now that I think about it, it seems to me that the moonlight did not appear until I lit a candle, or at least until I left the cottage. I call it a cottage, not knowing what the place really was.

I look back and notice the cottage disappearing in fog. I'm still frightened. What if I can't find my way back? I decide to return for at least a moment, get my bearings better, if possible. It feels uncomfortable but I do it anyway.

The fog begins to dissipate as I draw nearer to the cottage. I blink, shaking my head, almost unsurprised. The cottage is gone.

Which way can I possibly go now? Lost and alone at night, in a strange place, in a strange time, with strange clothes? And yet the feeling of desolation is not as over-whelming as it could be. I feel almost encouraged to know I truly must find my own way now. Nowhere to hide. No one to ask for guidance.

I continue along the road, looking for any sign of civilization. Nothing. Then, without warning, something appears: a gauzy light in the distance, dim yellow, but visible. A gentle wind blows, but it's not too cold, and I feel like I can make it there easily, though it's a long way away.

Walking and walking, taking seemingly forever to get even this close. Taking a long, long time to get a little closer. And finally, right when I'm starting to wonder whether it's a mirage, I see a building attached to the light, and I realize it's some kind of lamp outside a building—kerosene, maybe, or something like it.

When I reach the door to the house—for it is indeed a house, and a rather glamorous looking one—I stand outside for a few minutes, hearing the sound of voices within. They're undoubtedly British, but I cannot make out what they're saying. It seems presumptuous, perhaps even dangerous, to pick up the door knocker and expect to gain entrance among strangers. Yet I feel I must do something. Standing out here all night is not an option.

When the door opens, I'm confronted with an unfamiliar face, a man in his forties dressed much like myself. But unlike the situation with Ochs, surrounded by people who don't know me, this stranger's face lights up when he sees me.

"Sir Michael! Heaven forbid you should stand long in that cold night air. Come, come." He beckons me to enter, nodding and smiling.

So I am Sir Michael, and somehow I am known here. I smile and play along, hoping the right words will come…and that someone will use my host's name soon.

"Good evening, good evening," I say, picking up the pattern of his speech. "How nice to see you."

"Let me take your coat," he says. "We have some very special guests this evening."

"Oh, indeed?" I pretend to be surprised—of course, I have no idea, truly, who will be here, though I suspect I will soon meet Samuel Taylor Coleridge. But my opening gambit has the exact opposite effect on my host.

"Well, well, you are a deep one, are you not?" He chuckles. "Of course, you know Mr. Coleridge is here, and Mr. Hazlitt. You'll stay to dinner?"

"Certainly," I say. "I appreciate the hospitality."

Again he laughs, all good natured solicitude. "The pleasure is mine." He wheels around and calls out in the direction of an antechamber within, "Gentlemen. May I present Sir Michael."

And now a moment of dreadful, awkward silence as we enter the larger room adjacent to the antechamber. A banquet table stands covered with silver goblets and plates and all manner of food. But the awkwardness comes from the sudden movement of all the guests, standing to acknowledge me as if I were a great lady. This is a bit of etiquette that probably vanished from polite society in the late 1800s, though the tradition of standing for women remains in some quarters even to this day.

Flustered, I try to make a joke of it, not knowing how appropriate or inappropriate it may be. "Gentlemen, please, please. Don't get your old joints cracking on my account."

The eldest among them can't be more than forty, and the joke works. They erupt into laughter, seeming to loosen up from whatever weighty conversation they were having before I entered the room.

But my discomfort lingers, as I have to determine which guests know me and which do not. I leave it to the whim of my host, feeling I am somehow at his mercy. I scan the group for Coleridge, quickly realizing I will not recognize him from memory. I really don't know what he looks like.

"Sir Michael, may I present Mr. Hazlitt."

I smile and bow slightly in return.

My host goes around the group in order, naming each guest. He lands on Coleridge, and with a slight shock of recognition, I realize I've seen a painting of him. "And," he finishes, "of course you know me, the inevitable Josiah Wedgwood."

Again they laugh, and I feel as though I've dodged a bullet. Or maybe a musket ball.

I remain quiet during the meal, nodding here and there, listening to their conversation. After dinner we go for a walk, and I find myself walking side by side with Coleridge. As the rest of the group falls behind us, we get into a conversation about the artist's journey, a subject on which Coleridge has many ideas.

"If you've any familiarity with Schelling's philosophy of Nature, you must realize it leads inevitably to a theory of Art," he says. "I have been working at some length on a book on the subject and can only ascertain one incontrovertible principle: that there is a definite influence of the laws of the natural world on the ideas of human reason. There is some subtle, sympathetic relationship between them. Undoubtedly, the organic form is innate. It shapes itself from within, and the fullness of its development is one and the same with the perfection of its outward form. Such as the life is, such is the form. Nature, the prime, genial artist, inexhaustible in diverse powers, is equally inexhaustible in forms, is it not?"

"You are talking Plato."

"But so much more than Platonic theory!" he says, his voice rising. "It is Kant, and Goethe and Shakespeare and *every*body. In short, everyone and everything. All are connected. We hunger for eternity because there are eternal principles all round us. There are surely laws by which every aspect of existence is governed. And yet, to apprehend the absolute, to be at one with the immutable…what more worthy goal, and what more difficult task?"

This is Coleridge at his most formidable and most enthusiastic. Coming from the world I usually inhabit, it is hard to remember this man is in his mid-twenties. I try to keep in mind that only some of his questions are rhetorical, answering him in the most appropriate way I know how.

"Can you truly apprehend the absolute? Can you truly be at one with the immutable? Perhaps to attempt to do so is to risk annihilation."

Coleridge pauses. "Why annihilation?"

"What does it take to accomplish what you seek to accomplish? Can it really be done through intellect, or feeling?"

"I think it can, but one cannot yet be sure," he replies. "Perhaps it is more like what happens upon awakening from a dream. There is a profound sense, at times, of a kind of nostalgic longing, or of a recollection of some dim, obscure truth long forgotten…but before one is able to apprehend it, it recedes, like water into the shallows."

"That may be so, but what if it is only attainable through death?" I ask.

He stops walking, and I pull up short beside him. "Then I shall die trying to attain it," he says.

I take a deep breath, and then I quote him to his face:

For he hath tasted honey dew
And drunk the milk of paradise.

Coleridge looks directly at me, his eyes widening.

"Yes," I say, "I've read it."

"Sir, I am quite flattered indeed," he says. "Pray tell, wherever did you read my work?"

"It is indeed a mystery to myself how I know these lines," I say, feigning a poor memory. "I have read widely lately, and I know your name as well as your reputation, but I cannot recall the circumstance."

"As to our topic…perhaps there is another way."

"To be at one with the absolute?"

"Yes," he says. "Well, of course you have read Dr. Johnson?"

"Certainly."

"He once wrote, *The certainty that life cannot be long, and the probability that it will be much shorter than nature allows, ought to awaken every man to the active prosecution of whatever he is desirous to perform.* You agree?"

"It would be hard to argue against him, in that or any point."

We laugh.

"Have you ever taken laudanum?" he asks.

I pause. "It is a kind of tonic, as I understand it."

"Indeed. Sometimes…." His attention seems to wander, as if he is reliving the drug experience itself. "Sometimes it seems as if it is all a dream, other times, as if some sort of veil has been lifted. One wonders whether all of this is a dream…as Shakespeare said, all the world a stage, all of us players."

"Perhaps," I say. "But perhaps—" I hesitate, afraid to sound like I'm preaching at him "—perhaps it is merely a kind of trap."

"This world in which we dwell?"

"No, no—I meant the laudanum experiment."

He looks at me, and something in his face closes like a door. "I think it more likely a vehicle. A kind of experiment, as you say, yes, but…an experimental technique for *expanding* consciousness, not trapping it."

He smiles coolly, and I see I have lost him. Of course. Foolish of me to push the issue so far so fast. What addict, seeing a potential threat to his addiction, would not vigorously defend it?

"Forgive me," I say in my most studiously polite British manner. "I did not intend to imply *you* were trapped by it. Quite obviously, it has proven immensely useful for you. I only wondered whether it might have a limited application, as it were. In other words, if it might eventually prove to be unhelpful."

"You haven't ever taken it, have you?" he asks.

I can see a potential for conflict here if I admit I haven't. I look away.

"Actually, I have," I say, "but I found it did not agree with my constitution. My stomach reacted badly to it. But I think I understand what you may have experienced… 'the lifting of the veil,' and so on."

"Yes," he says. "Yes." And he falls uncharacteristically silent, no doubt longing for Mistress Laudanum, still certain I do not truly understand.

For the moment, we are walking and making no eye contact, distant now. I'd felt close to him, somehow, as this encounter is lasting much longer than those with Ochs and Faulkner. Perhaps that's why I say, without thinking, "If you don't stop, you'll become an addict."

"What?"

Everything snaps to a halt. I glance back in Coleridge's direction, and he's frozen in place, everyone and everything around him frozen in place—no wind in the trees, no clouds moving. No sound. At the exact moment of this sudden freeze, David appears just beyond Coleridge. He and I are the only beings who move in this frozen world.

"What are you doing?" he asks.

"I—I don't know."

"Come on," he says. "I've got to get you out of here."

SEVEN

WE SLEEP AGAIN, OR SO IT SEEMS. But when I awaken, we are back in that same room—not the hotel-like one, the eighteenth-century one. I see David is already up, assuming he's even slept.

"How are you feeling?" he asks.

I stretch. "I'm okay, I think. What's happening? Why are we still here?"

"There's a problem."

I look at him and see how much more serious than a six-year-old he looks. In fact, I've never seen him this serious before. "What's wrong? Is it because...I started to tell Coleridge he's an addict?"

"Not only that. You know what you were about to tell him?"

I have to stop and think. At first, I'm not even sure what I said, much less what I was going to say. But then it hits me. "That if he didn't stop, it would have a profound negative impact on his life. Wow. Damn, that's what I was about to tell him."

"Right. You can't do that. That's actually the opposite of what you're supposed to do. So we've got trouble. I mean, *you've* got trouble."

Now he really has my attention. I sit up in bed. "What do you mean?"

"You understand we're doing all this in our sleep, right?"

"We are?"

Finally, he relaxes a bit, and chuckles. "Remember when we started? I told you sometimes I sleep through the night like normal kids, but most nights I'm off on one of these little excursions?"

"Right, right. I remember being surprised you knew the word *excursions*. Sorry," I say when I see his withering look. "Seems like a long time ago. So we're going back to our normal lives shortly. All this has happened through the course of one night."

"Exactly," he says. "The part about this happening in the course of a night. But the normal lives part—that's where there's a problem."

"So are you saying I'm stuck here?"

He looks down, then back up. "I don't know," he admits. "This hasn't happened before, as far as I know. There's a word you adults use—unprecedented, I think?"

I heave a sigh. "Oh, man. I wasn't thinking. You're not stuck, though, right? You said *I've* got trouble, not you."

"Right, I'm not stuck. But I don't want to leave you here. I'm not sure when you'll be out. Saying what you said—and starting to say what you were about to say—I guess there's a chance it could have changed history."

"I understand. David, I'm sorry. You don't need to stay with me. Go back when you can. I haven't forgotten, you're a kid."

"It's okay," he says. "I'm fine for the moment. But I do have to get back to school."

"All right. I'll be fine. You go ahead."

He closes his eyes, then opens them again and looks at me. "Do me a favor, okay?"

"What's that?"

"I'm going to try something. When I close my eyes, close your eyes too. If I can take you with me, I will. If not, I'll be back with you as soon as I can."

"Sure."

"Don't open them until I say something, okay?"

"Okay."

He closes his eyes and I follow suit. Silence. I don't think anything has happened at first, but somehow I sense a shift of energy in the room…like I'm alone.

I wait for him to say something, but he doesn't. I think he's gone and I'm stuck here, but I'm not a hundred percent sure. He did say, *Don't open them until I say something.* He's said nothing. Is he gone?

I'm almost sure he's gone. The room is deadly quiet, and yet I'm not convinced I am alone.

Finally, after what seems a ridiculously long period of

time, I open my eyes. I blink against the unnatural brightness of the room. David is gone. At least he's not where he was before.

Still, I don't quite feel like I'm alone. I feel as if there's some other presence in the room, and the feeling is not creepy or scary—it's actually good—but it makes me a little nervous.

"So," I say aloud to myself, "that's that. Now I guess I sit here alone. Only God knows for how long."

"God isn't the only one who knows," says a voice from behind me, and a sickening chill of fear and shock runs through me. I wheel around.

"You didn't expect to find me here, did you?" the Coordinator asks. "It's all right. Please compose yourself."

I take a deep breath, let it out slowly. No doubt I'm glaring at him, sitting there in his long gold robe, like no one has glared since he was a normal human being on earth… assuming he ever *was* a normal human being. "You know you just scared the living shit out of me, don't you?"

"Not my intention at all," he says, rising. "Although I must say, you showed remarkable self-restraint, including in those moments after David was gone. It's a pity you were unable to restrain yourself equally during your encounter with Mr. Coleridge."

I feel myself flush. "I know. I feel badly about that, though my admittedly limited understanding is Coleridge won't remember any of our discussion anyway."

"True," says the Coordinator. "True, but hardly the point. You remember the instructions you received at the outset?"

"*Don't try to change the course of history.* I understand. And again, I am sorry. I got caught up in—"

"Do you recall the rest of the instructions? The potential consequences?"

"I could get stuck here?"

"Yes. My exact words were, *You won't change history, of course. There might be dire consequences for you if you tried.* In this case, that means your best-case scenario would be running the risk of getting stuck in eighteenth-century England."

"A risk I just ran."

"Precisely. Do you like it here?"

Now I feel even more disturbed, though I'm not sure what he's really asking. "I find it fascinating, but—what do you mean, do I like it?"

"Would you be comfortable staying here indefinitely? None of the comforts of the twenty-first century you've grown accustomed to: indoor plumbing, smartphones, recorded music...."

"You're serious. Am I trapped here? Is that a threat, a punishment? What?"

"Not at all. I think you get the idea, and should be able to restrain yourself from making a comparable mistake during future ventures. Are you ready to go?"

He looks at me without any discernible emotion, and I'm not sure if that's really an invitation or not. I decide to treat it as one. "Yes. Yes, I'm ready to go."

"Good. We'll leave in a moment. One other thing: I also told you that you will have to content yourself at first with following David, and David will then have to content himself with following you. Do you remember that?"

"Yes."

"You followed David twice. To New York City and then—"

"Mississippi, yes. Phil Ochs and Faulkner."

"Correct. Then David followed you here. You noticed you thought yourself alone here at first?"

"Yes, I did."

"Because of what has just happened—what you did—you will have to follow David again. Only this time it will be on one of his excursions, where you simply observe. Call it a demotion."

"That seems fair. Where are we going?"

"The Children's Cancer Center at Florida Hospital."

EIGHT

AND WITH THAT, I'M GONE AGAIN AND REAPPEAR
AGAIN WITHOUT WARNING OR EVEN THE ABILITY TO
DO ANYTHING ABOUT IT. But I remember what he said,
this Coordinator person, or whatever he is, and I'm not
happy about it.

To make matters even worse, he's still with me—apparently we're invisible to everyone else, but the Coordinator
sits right beside me. I see David at the bedside of a smaller
boy up ahead. The hospital's antiseptic smell engulfs me
even before I open my mouth to speak.

"Oh no. I can't—I mean, I'm not good with stuff like this. I can't handle it. Seriously."

"That's all right," he says. "You're here only as an observer. Besides, David is much stronger than you."

I glare at the Coordinator again. He watches as David and the boy speak in low whispers, and of course it's true: they certainly don't need my help or interference. The six-year-old *is* stronger than me.

The Coordinator glances over, picking up on the glare. But he doesn't seem to be troubled by it, or even judge it. He nods back in the direction of the two boys as if to let me know that's where I should focus my attention.

Without any particular intention I slowly rise, slowly begin to walk toward David and the other boy. The Coordinator walks close behind me, gliding silently along. We pause and stand back a short distance from the bed.

"What do you think?" David asks. "You know you're going to be okay?"

"I know I'm going to die," the boy says matter-of-factly. "So no, I guess I'm not."

"I mean after that," David says. "You know everything's going to be all right, don't you?"

The boy's blue eyes flash up and fix on David. "What do you mean?"

"Your parents will grieve. They'll cry, and have a hard time sleeping, and not really be able to do much at work for a while. But they won't die for a long time. They'll be okay. And when you die, you'll be okay too."

"How do you know all this?" the boy asks.

"I just do," David says. "When you die, you go somewhere else. You'll like it better than here. You ever have dreams at night where you're flying?"

The boy tilts his head and smiles. "Yeah. Those are the best."

David smiles back. "It's like that. You're going to fly and fly and fly. Over hills and trees and clouds and even birds. You won't ever feel pain again."

"Really?"

David nods slowly, the smile fading. "Really. You remember all those things about heaven your parents told you? Angels with harps and all that?"

"Yeah."

"That would be boring for you, but don't worry—it's not like that at all. It's adventure when you want, and rest when you want. And you'll feel fine…all the time."

The boy reaches up and takes David's hand. My eyes blur with hot tears, and I can't see either of them clearly as he says, "Thank you. That helps a lot."

"Thank *you*," David says. "You've helped me more than I could ever help you."

"How is that possible?"

"You'll see," says David. "I'm pretty sure you'll find out soon enough."

I have to turn away, as I hear myself sob loudly.

The Coordinator looks over at me but does not move. I walk back a few paces, then turn away from them once more.

And then, again, like lightning the Coordinator is gone.

NINE

I'M STUNNED NOW INTO A LONGER SILENCE. I can't talk to the boy, can't talk to David, can't talk to the Coordinator. He's gone. Or is he?

I wonder, what does this Coordinator person know? What does he plan for us, if anything? Over whom or what does his power extend? Over whom or what *doesn't* his power extend? It's all a mystery.

David and the boy are still talking behind me. I look back. I can't do it. I can't "observe" them any longer. The hot tears that rose to my eyes have already run down my cheeks, leaving cool trails. I wipe each cheek with the back of my hand.

I have to get out of here.

I start walking, but of course I don't know where I'm going. I've never been to this hospital, I don't even know what year it is…or if I'm really me, or some other version. I don't care at this point. I need some air.

I follow the exit signs, unable—or unwilling, anyway—to talk to anyone. The long white corridors, like any facility, have no personality. There are no real guideposts or landmarks in such a place. Eventually I find an exit and see daylight ahead.

When the Florida humidity hits me, I breathe out automatically…and realize I've been holding my breath as I walk, not wanting to inhale any more of the antiseptic stench of the hospital. I stand in place a moment, inhaling and exhaling. Almost gasping. I don't know how I'm even going to get my bearings, not knowing what the time frame is, what my next move is supposed to be. Presumably I'm supposed to shadow David until we go somewhere else, but I can't even handle that right now.

I feel I have failed already.

I look to my left and right. The parking lot goes on for miles, it seems. Do I have a car? I have keys in my pocket and I pull them out to look at them.

Then I hear a voice over my shoulder.

"Don't worry."

The Coordinator. So he's not gone. I turn around. "Don't worry? Did you actually just say 'Don't worry' to me? You realize this kid is going to die from cancer, right? I mean, that's why we're here, isn't it?"

"Yes," he says. "Yes, it is. And of course you understand this is a privilege…especially for someone as young as David?"

"I suppose I can see that, yes."

"You know, less than one tenth of one percent of the population of the world will ever be granted such a privilege—in any incarnation."

I see he's letting that sink in, and indeed I pause before replying. "What do you mean, in any incarnation?"

His eyes flicker, a look I can't read. "Ah, of course. You're American. You are familiar with the concept of reincarnation?"

"Yes, but it's only a theory. No one really knows if there is such a thing."

"Now you know there is such a thing. You can take it as a fact of existence. Not a theory."

"You're telling me we're reincarnated beings? We've had previous lives?"

"Not necessarily life such as you know it, but yes, previous incarnations. That is indeed a fact. But then you already sense this about yourself, do you not?"

I have to admit I do. "Yes, I've often wondered what sort of bad karma I might be trying to burn off in this life."

For the first time in maybe forever, I watch the corners of the Coordinator's mouth turn upward into a slight smile. "I see," he says simply. "If you'd done all that badly, you wouldn't even be here. So there is that."

"Yes," I say. "There is that."

We pause, sizing each other up. Or no, that's not quite right either. I size him up, yes, again. But he is looking at me with, it seems, some slight bemusement and something I had not recognized from him before: compassion.

"So, what's our next move?"

"I think you've seen everything you need to see here,"

he says. "I do believe you have another trip into the past ahead of you."

With that, we are both gone again.

TEN

I AWAKE STARTLED, RESTED, ALONE. No Coordinator, no David. I'm in that hotel room again, so at least I know I'm not back in the eighteenth century. The strange pointillist-style painting hangs on the wall opposite the bed as always. I stand and walk toward it and see immediately that it has quite a few more dots in various places than the last version. It's almost uncanny how much it's begun to look like more than simple abstract dots. I'm convinced it must mean something, though I can't imagine what.

I head into the bathroom to freshen up before I even attempt to go out to whatever sort of world I'm in now. Here

I notice something different. This *isn't* the same hotel-style room. Or if it is, it's an older version. It smells different, though I can't say how exactly. The bathroom mirror has a cool, vintage-looking frame around it, the plumbing fixtures are old school—1950s, maybe even 1940s. Who will I meet next? Billie Holiday? Another writer, like Fitzgerald or Hemingway? I wonder as I wash up.

On my way back into the bedroom, I realize I could check my personal belongings first to get the lay of the land. I pull my wallet off the side table and look through it, but I'm surprised: it's my regular real-life wallet, with my current cards. There's only a dollar in it, so that's not great. Having seen myself in the mirror a moment ago, I know I'm me again. I'm in my fifties, balding with glasses and a driver's license that doesn't expire for another seven years. Wherever I've landed in the twentieth century, it looks like I'm not going to need ID.

The first thing I notice on my way out the door is I don't have a key. I check my own keychain, and again, it's normal: house key, mailbox key, the black plastic key fob for my Honda Accord. I presume I'd better keep both wallet and keys hidden in my pockets. The key fob would look like something that operates a spaceship to anyone in this era, and the wallet was made by Ralph Lauren—a guy who didn't even form a company until the late 1960s.

I know when I close the heavy door behind me I'll be locked out, alone and unsure where to go, much less where I'll sleep next. I don't know if I'll meet up with David, though I can't expect it. No idea what happened to the Coordinator either. I imagine I'll have to go with the flow and trust the process—something that's never been my strong suit, but I can probably do it here. I doubt I have any other choice.

I close the door, and outside it's exactly as I expected: a hotel, Howard Johnson style, with a small, generic parking lot. Not many cars, but the styles signal I'm between where I was before, around 1966, and where I was before that, circa 1928. Not quite 1960s yet, but firmly in the twentieth century. If this is a place I've been before, it's a version that existed before I was born.

It feels like autumn in New England. The leaves are turning red and yellow, and some have even reached that color of rolled, rusted wire I remember from childhood, passing hayfields in my parents' car. The memory comes back with unusual force as I walk across the lot, looking for something familiar.

And then I see it: the clock. It's on a hill adjacent to the street I stand on now, a white clock atop a tall black metal pole with a wide base. The face of the clock reads *United Bank & Trust Co.* It stands beneath a low underpass that looks like an old railroad trestle, near the corner of Main and Prospect Street.

I'm in Bristol, Connecticut, my hometown, right in front of the old Bristol Bank & Trust. Born here in 1964, I now stand across from an intersection knowing the time is at least a few years before I was born. Somewhere around here are my parents, maybe newlyweds. My grandparents are all still alive in this world. The throng of feelings and thoughts takes my breath away, and I have to sit down, right on the curb by the street corner. I don't know whether to be traumatized or overwhelmed with gratitude.

I know I'm here, but I don't know why or precisely when. No one is coming to assist me, from what I can see—no Coordinator, no sign of David or anyone else. There's hardly anyone around, in fact. Only a few strangers walking into shops in the distance, unaware of me and certainly not at all interested.

Without thinking, I walk down Riverside Avenue then head to the corner of North Street and North Main, about a mile altogether. There I find myself in front of an unfamiliar old fifties-style diner, except its name is one I used to hear all the time when I was a kid: the Palace of Sweets. Adults spoke lovingly of it from their childhoods, as if it were some kind of amazing Willie Wonka tableau, with homemade fudge and jawbreakers and jellied candies standing in row upon row behind domed glass. But it turns out it was only a diner—gleaming metal and barstools and a soda fountain, with a few items of homemade candy for sale.

When I walk in, it's the tail end of lunch time. The place smells of hamburgers and fries. A handful of people stand in the back speaking to each other in Greek, which makes the experience even stranger. Growing up in Bristol, I never heard people speaking any language other than English.

I sit at the counter and a man comes over. I order a Coke. He looks at me curiously, as if wondering whether I'm new in town. Maybe he sees a relative of mine in my appearance. Maybe it's my clothes, a little out of place in the fifties, though not unusual enough to draw excessive attention.

When I pull out the Ralph Lauren wallet, I remember I didn't want anyone to see it. But the Coke is less than a dollar anyway, so handing over a single dollar bill won't attract much attention. The wallet is black, not really as noticeable as I'd thought.

"Sorry," I say. "I don't have any change on me."

He grunts, takes the dollar, hands me my change. Shiny new quarters and pennies dated 1952, 1955. I put them into my pocket casually, sensing it's as surreal as hanging out with Coleridge, Faulkner, Phil Ochs.

Two young women walk in and sit at the counter a few barstools down. They look to be in their early twenties, a blonde and a brunette. Now I feel more self-conscious. They're dressed in the long skirts and blouses common to the era, and my clothes really do look foreign in contrast to theirs.

I don't recognize the blonde at all, but the woman with the dark brown hair is not completely unfamiliar somehow. She reminds me a bit of a younger version of my grandmother on my father's side, though of course I never knew her when she was anywhere near that young.

As I think this, the dark-haired woman says, "I don't suppose there's any way I can get a highball in this place, is there?"

"Janie," the blonde says, and gives her a little shove. "You're so bad. Besides, it's too early in the day to be thinking of a drink."

"I don't know about that," Janie says, and with a shock of recognition I freeze in my seat. Janie. My Aunt Jane, my father's sister. My favorite aunt.

She's only in her early twenties, barely more than a kid. She can't be over twenty-four, the age I'll be when I get sober in 1989.

She will die of alcoholism at the age of forty. And there's not a goddamn thing I can do about it.

I'm still frozen at the counter, glancing sideways but otherwise paralyzed. She can't possibly recognize me no matter what I say or do, because I haven't even been born yet. She hasn't cradled me in her arms yet. But it's definitely possible she'll see a family resemblance of one sort or another, although I take after my mother's side more in appearance.

Janie and her blonde friend order root beer floats, and I glance over again, trying not to get caught. These two twenty-somethings would be creeped out by a man in his fifties looking at them.

But it's too late. We're the only three customers and noticing me is inevitable. I look down at my brown leather jacket and jeans and understand how out of place they are in this town at this time. I haven't exactly transformed the way I did for Coleridge and his peers.

"Excuse me, sir," the blonde girl says. "Do you have the time?"

I instinctively reach for my cell phone, but it's not there in my pocket. The girls eye me as I pull my right hand back out but then look down at my left wrist. I'm surprised to see I'm wearing a watch I hadn't noticed earlier. "It's ten after twelve," I say.

"See?" the blonde says to Jane, and turns back to me with a perfunctory, "Thank you." Then back to Jane. "It's barely past noon."

Jane heaves a sigh. "I know. I don't feel good, though."

"Well, a highball wouldn't make it better, would it?"

Again, Jane says, "I don't know about that."

"What's wrong?"

"You know I don't have any arches in my feet, right?"

"Sure," the blonde says. "I remember."

"So they're flat and they hurt. A lot. And I've got problems with my teeth. I feel like I'm hypersensitive. I get really nervous. Sometimes I even break out in hives. Look at this."

She pulls up a sleeve, revealing a pink forearm.

"That's not from the feet, is it?"

Another sigh. "No. I don't know. I don't think so. I wish I could fix them, though. My feet. I heard about this operation where they place an artificial arch in each foot. If I had the money, I'd get it. You ever hear of that?"

"No," the blonde says.

They lower their voices to whispers. I can't hear what they're saying, and doubt I'd be any help even if I could. I finish my Coke and signal the man back behind the counter as if he were a bartender. "Another," I say.

At length, the blonde friend leaves and my Aunt Jane is alone. She sighs again.

"Hey kid," I say. "Talk to you for a minute?"

She looks over at me. "Yes sir."

"Let's get a booth, okay?"

She eyes me with suspicion. "Okay."

We move from the barstools at the counter to a booth by the window.

"Listen," I say. "I don't know how to tell you this. I don't know what to say. But there's something I have to tell you."

She says, "What is it? Who are you?"

I look at her, overwhelmed with compassion. "You don't recognize me, do you?"

"No," she says. "Should I?"

"Your name is Jane, right?"

"Yes."

"What's your last name?"

She tells me.

"Mine too," I say.

"You're a relative?"

"That's what I want to tell you," I say.

"Oh. Are you one of the uncles?"

"No. Let me ask you another question: have you ever wanted to go to California?"

"Of course," she says. "Every Connecticut kid wants to escape to California."

"Right. Tell me something: do you have a girlfriend?"

She colors. "Girlfriend? Everyone's got girlfriends. You mean a boyfriend?"

I shake my head. "No. I mean a girlfriend."

She makes a move as if to escape.

"No, wait. It's okay," I say. "I understand."

She slumps down slightly in the booth. "Who are you?" she says.

"I'm going to tell you, but I need to ask you to remain very calm."

"Okay."

"Can you do that for me?"

She nods. She looks frightened.

"I'm your nephew, Mike."

She laughs in disbelief. "What?"

"I'm going to be your brother's son. His second son. You're my aunt."

Her brow furrows. "That's impossible."

"I know," I say, "I know. It's all crazy to me, too. I'm back here in my hometown before I was born. And right now I'm already old enough to be your father. But when I'm actually born, you're already an adult.

"My parents are going to get married, if they're not married already. And they're going to have my brother, and he's going to look like you. And then they're going to have me."

I see a shiver run through her, and I realize in that moment she believes I'm telling the truth. Somehow she knows I'm telling the truth.

"Oh my God."

"Yes," I say.

"How do I know you're who you say you are? From the future and all that. It's crazy. It's impossible."

"Want me to name some names?" I ask. "Your parents, your brothers? My mother?"

"Yeah."

I name them, watching her face as the doubt that momentarily crept in creeps back out.

"How are you here?" she asks. "How did this all happen?"

"It's a long story," I tell her, "and I don't really have any answers. I don't know what I'm doing here either. And I'm trying to do the next right thing, but I have a tendency to get in trouble."

"So okay. You know my family, and my brother's girlfriend. I still don't know you are who you say you are."

I sigh. I feel like I should be accomplishing more, like we're wasting time. "Look," I say, "I've been to some other places, and I was always equipped to fit in. Somehow, I haven't been this time. Check this out." I pull out my key fob for the 2016 Honda.

"What is that?"

"It's a security system to open a car in the future. The top button locks the door, the middle button opens it, and the bottom one opens the trunk."

"Holy shit." She giggles, covering her mouth. "I'm sorry."

"You don't have to apologize to me for that," I say. "Sounds like I take after you."

We both laugh.

"So you don't know why you're here? You don't have some mission you've been sent to fulfill?"

"I guess I do, but I don't receive instructions. You're going to see me again in a few years, but I won't remember it. And you won't remember meeting me, either."

"But that's sad."

I nod. "I think so too. But something is happening here. I've gone from meeting people I admire to meeting people from my own life. It's like I'm getting closer and closer to something, something I should be reaching for but never have. I don't know what it is. I don't understand it myself."

She nods, too, slowly, sadly. In that moment, I see her future so clearly, her inevitable downward trajectory, her premature death, and the combination of empathy and sympathy and sadness drives a chill up my spine and tears into my eyes.

"What's wrong?"

I sob, then swallow it. The staff in the corner of the diner look over at me—curious, concerned.

"You've got to stop," I tell her, taking her hand.

"Stop?"

I look down at the table. "Drinking," I say. "It's killing your father, it's killing you—" I glance up and see where the Coordinator stands in the corner of the diner, glaring, right before everything goes black.

ELEVEN

I AM DREAMING. It's a nightmare, one I've had before, one so lifelike I cannot recall, in waking moments, how many times this has happened in dreams and how many in real life. It is as if I am walking down the darkened hallway in the house of my youth toward the black maw of the open bedroom door, each nerve straining with the knowledge that every sound, every creak of a floorboard, might awaken my father and incur his displeasure. He has taught me too well that the mild-mannered facade he so effortlessly presents when sober can dissolve into a towering rage at the least provocation, and as I tiptoe down the long dark carpet, the adrenalin rush buoys me up like a sparrow on an upsurge of wind and I feel, in spite of the terror that envelops me, fantastic.

Without warning the door at the far end of the hall swings open, a dark shape in the dark distance, and sheer terror overcomes me. I feel I will void my bladder or bowels, or both, like someone does when they are about to be killed. From a great distance above me, I hear the word, *Defiance.*

I freeze. "What?"

Bolt upright in bed, slamming from dark into light, and there sits the Coordinator with an old, old man with a long grey beard in a soft white robe.

"What?" I say, still gasping.

"Denial. Defiance. Insanity: doing the same thing over and over but expecting different results."

"Really? Is that what you're going to do? Punish me with platitudes?" I spit each word out, hard on the letter *p.* Peter Piper picked a peck of pickled peppers. Fuck it. "Who's he?" I say, gesturing to the old man.

"You already know," the Coordinator says, and in that moment I understand. David mentioned him, a lifetime ago, it seems now. He's a wizard of some kind, and my own spirit guide, though I'd long since forgotten him, ignored him, pretended he didn't exist. A mere figment of my imagination.

"M'Extezuh," I say.

The old man grins when he hears me pronounce his name. He stands up.

"My dear boy," he says. "It's been a long, long time since you sought me, has it not?"

"Yes," I say, not meeting his eyes. "I'm sorry."

"You do not owe me an apology," he says. "Do you remember how you met me?"

I look up again, this time into his eyes, which are periwinkle blue. "In meditation. I sought a spirit guide, and you appeared."

"Yes, and we spoke many times in your meditations. Do you remember?" He sits down again, folds his hands in his lap.

"A little," I say. "I'm sure I've forgotten most of it."

He nods, still smiling. "Shall we discuss attachment today?"

"Is that what this is? You two are going to give me a lecture about detaching with love?"

M'Extezuh's smile disappears. "It is unfortunate you are angered by this gift you have been given. Would you like to talk about it more?"

"Not really."

He nods again. "To follow the peaceful way is to receive both good and bad with the same spirit of equanimity as that with which the ocean receives rain."

"I'm no ocean," I tell him. "I'm only human. And that was my aunt—my *dead* aunt."

"You know," M'Extezuh says, "I am not some disembodied spirit who never knew a human form. I come from the same world as you. I, too, had to learn things the hard way: that in giving up attachment to individuals, and to the material world, I become not poorer but richer. In dropping the manacles of self, am I not today unfettered?"

"I don't know. I guess so. You wandered pretty freely into my meditations back in the day."

"Yes, and that was from freedom to travel the spirit world—not during life, but after living. Such is the cat who sheds his winter coat in spring, and it is a rare person indeed who looks at him strangely."

For some reason, this cracks me up, and in that moment it seems as if all three of us breathe a sigh of relief. I notice a mischievous glint in the old man's eyes.

"Well, your heart was in the right place," he says. "Your head was in another orifice, but…"

Even the Coordinator laughs at that one, and M'Extezuh stands up again.

"I get it," I say. "At least, I think I do."

"Then we shall speak of this another time. I will leave you to it."

He disappears, which at this point doesn't even faze me. Just another day in the spirit world, I guess.

I sigh, looking over at The Coordinator again.

"So now what? Back to David?"

He stands, slowly. "I'm afraid it's not that simple. You see, the experience with Coleridge was unfortunate but understandable. However, this second time is a more serious transgression. I am only something of an enforcer in this situation, not a decision maker."

"What do you mean?"

He turns to me. "Your last action may have prevented you from ever returning to normal life."

I leap off the bed. "How can my life ever *be* normal again after all this? What are you even talking about? It's like all riddles and hocus pocus with you. Can't you talk to me like a normal person instead of like some kind of condescending guru? Seriously. Do you even have a name? Because I've never heard one."

He sighs, looking away. "It is of no consequence. I know you originally thought of me simply as 'the man in the golden robe,' and then as 'the Coordinator,' after David's introduction. The fact is, I am a kind of afterlife functionary. M'Extezuh, who truly is your spirit guide, operates in a much higher realm than me."

"So he's like a vice president, and you're what? A clerk?"

The Coordinator turns his baleful gaze on me, and this time it no longer seems neutral. For the first time, I feel as though it is full of venom…as though, in this strange unsettling no-man's-land between life and death, I am not walking among purely friendly beings.

"At your current level of understanding, you could look at it that way," he says. "Although I would describe my position as something more like what you think of as middle management."

"So there's a pecking order? And M'Extezuh is above you, but he just pussied out because you get the task of doing what—delivering some kind of punishment? You know what, bring it on. I don't even care at this point. I care a hell of a lot more about my Aunt Jane than I do about you, or even the old man."

Whatever venom I thought I saw dissipates as he again looks at me with what I can only describe as compassion. "I hope you will not view these consequences as punishment. You know, out of the worst of times, you have always grown stronger, and good things have come from what looked like bad things. Do you remember the year you turned forty-seven?"

"Of course. Worst year of my life. I suppose you know all about it. You know everything about me, right? Past, present, future?"

"No," he says, "only the past. I know nothing definite of your current state of mind, although I can surmise it. I know still less of your future. But I know about that year. You developed tinnitus, ringing in your ears. Your wife of nearly a decade left you. I know you have told the story many times. You always use the phrase 'my wife of nine point five years—but who's counting?' Correct?"

I laugh bitterly. "Right. What else?"

"You then fell and broke your ankle during a five-kilometer run. The plumbing and air conditioning systems in your home leaked, leading to holes in your downstairs ceiling. You contemplated both bankruptcy and foreclosure, though you ultimately chose neither. And you developed nonmalignant masses in your face and neck that required major surgery, which left you with a large scar on your neck. I believe that about covers it."

"Yeah, I didn't have time for any more disasters that year."

He laughs gently. "You remember wanting to die, though, don't you?"

"Yes. I hadn't felt that low in over twenty years. I figured I'd had a pretty good run, and if I died in my sleep, that would have been fine by me. I wanted out of all the pain. Who wouldn't?"

"Indeed. And yet you survived. You continued to work. You paid your bills. You even tried to find love again, and ultimately succeeded."

Now I feel my eyes well up with tears. "And as I'm sure you know, I always say if I hadn't made it through all that, I wouldn't have met my second wife. I wouldn't have the happiness in my life I have today. I know."

"So out of the greatest suffering has come the greatest life has to offer you. That has been your experience in many ways, yes?"

"Pain as the touchstone of spiritual growth. Yes. I could do with a little less pain, and maybe that would mean a little less growth, but yes. That's my experience."

The Coordinator looks at me with something I can't quite read: a challenge, maybe, or a desire to push me. Something like that, I think. And then he says it. "That's why I think you're ready to handle the fact that your actions with your Aunt Jane may have prevented you from returning to normal life."

"But what does that even mean? I'm not going home to my wife? I'm stuck here with you? Stuck in the past?"

"As I began to tell you, I am not even sure myself. These types of infractions, or rebellious actions, are almost entirely without precedent. You understand, of course, time is an illusion. It's meaningless here."

"I don't think I do understand that, no. I don't think I understand much of anything anymore."

"When you go to sleep at night, it seems it's only for a few moments. You don't recall falling asleep—and even if you wake during the night, your consciousness prevents you from accurately tracking the passage of time. A lengthy, complex dream that actually takes a couple of hours may seem like ten or fifteen minutes at most. Does that sound about right?"

"Yeah, I think so. Sure."

"And you have dreamt you were flying before. Those are among the best dreams you've ever had, are they not?"

"They are, yes. That's true."

"You understand all of this is taking place while you are asleep? Your body is back in bed while you meet with me, with Phil Ochs, David, your aunt…everyone."

"Okay."

"In some ways, your sense of time here is more truly distorted than it is when you're sleeping. We could go—you and I, together—to many different realms throughout the universe, and in your perception it would take days, even weeks. But in the reality of your body, it would all happen within the space of a few hours. You are still in effect sleeping, while your mind is awake here."

"So I am confused, then. Am I in two places at once? I sure as heck have a body now. I'm inhabiting it."

"Yes, it's very much like what you call an out-of-body experience. Except, as you say, it's not out of the body entirely. You *are* in two places at once. Your mind is here, and back in that bed you are not even dreaming. All your consciousness is here…and it's going to be here for a while."

Now I can feel my own brow furrow. "How long is 'a while?'"

"Again, I don't know. But I think you are going to have to meditate on it alone. If you can meditate long enough here without feeling as though you are falling asleep, you may actually meet M'Extezuh again and speak with him one on one. But I truly do not know what will happen next. I know about the past, as I said, but the future direction is as much a mystery to me as it is to you."

TWELVE

AND SO I FIND MYSELF ON A STRANGE BED IN A STRANGE ROOM ALONE—CROSS-LEGGED, SILENT, MEDITATING. Eyes closed, back as straight as I can comfortably make it.

It's been a long time since I tried this particular meditation, but it makes sense, in light of the Coordinator's words. I picture myself in a place I used to call The Sanctuary, which in my case is at the top of Kent Falls in Connecticut. I used to go there often during meditation, and I grew somewhat skilled at conjuring the atmosphere in my mind, the sense of peace above the roar of the waterfall. It was there I first met the mysterious M'Extezuh. I'd read of meeting a spirit animal—that didn't ever seem to happen—and also of meeting a spirit guide, who could come in a human form, though not necessarily. I could vaguely picture the old man in my mind. He looked something like an actual historical figure, a guru named Sri Yukteswar.

I struggle to get to the spot on the Falls, but then I feel like I have a sense of it. The sound, even the smell. I imagine a warm day, a handful of white clouds in a sunny blue sky. In my mind, I hear the sound of the waterfall below. I do not have a mantra, but I use M'Extezuh's name as one.

"M'Extezuh." Nothing. "M'Extezuh. Are you there?"

"I am here." The answer comes in not like a voice, but rather a thought—a thought slightly stronger than any I could conjure on my own.

"I don't see you," I say. "Are you going to appear to me? Will we talk, as we did in the old days?"

"No," he says. "Not yet. You are not ready yet. You are not open."

It's true. There is a kind of ring of self-protection around me, like a gauzy wall. I've built it up in the years since I met M'Extezuh last—through the divorce, through job loss, illness, the ups and downs of life.

"What should I do?"

"Nothing," he says. "Be nothing. Do nothing. Have nothing."

I focus my attention on the space between the eyebrows, the Third Eye. I let go of something—pain, fear, anger… something intangible but somehow hard. I feel it go, and in that moment I feel something open. I try to maintain my focus on the space between my brows, but the feeling of profound relief is so overwhelming, I want to cry with happiness. I even sense a shift in my head, as the constant ringing in my ears that has plagued me for years drops down to a more tolerable level.

"That's better," says M'Extezuh. And in my mind's eye, he comes forward through what I imagine to be a stand of pine trees. "Now we can speak like men."

Somehow this amuses me, and I feel myself smile without actually laughing aloud. I hear his laughter, though—a great, laughing love.

"What do I need to do, M'Extezuh? What can I bring to this experience?"

"My son, you are one who repeats patterns," he says. "You have a history of self-defeating behavior. You know this about yourself. But like a musician practicing scales, you often repeat something because you are so accustomed to repeating it. And this has just happened now, with this rare and precious gift you have received of bringing comfort to suffering souls from the past. Rather than accept it graciously and stay in the moment, appreciating it for what it is, you have sought to control it—like a child with a dove. Rather than letting it fly freely, and risk that it might fly away too soon, you have strangled it. You understand?"

"Yes."

"Perhaps it began after meeting Phil, when you spoke with William. You told him he was going to be very famous. Do you remember?"

"Yes."

"In that way, you almost began to tell him too much. You were still overawed by The Coordinator, and ready and willing to obey him, or even David, at the merest suggestion or signal. You remember that as well?"

"Yes," I say again.

"Then you tried to change the course of history—first with Coleridge, then, more grievously, with your Aunt Jane. I know you remember all of this."

"I do."

"Now you must go back into the past again, into the world of another of your relations. You cannot—you must not—try to change that past. You are there to bring comfort, not control; to empathize, not fix. Again, do you understand?"

"Yes."

"Everything you need is already here. Everything that will ever happen has already happened. Every moment, past, present, and future, exists right now. There is nothing to gain or lose. Can you sense that here, in this state of awareness?"

"I think so, yes."

"Then let us go."

THIRTEEN

BOOM. Again, I fall into a past I may not recognize or even understand. I'm in the room again—so much like a hotel, it's not even funny. I turn to my right, and sure enough, the ever-present pointillist-style painting sits above my line of vision. I stand and walk toward it, riveted by the unusual number of new dots in the pattern.

I can finally tell the shape it forms is that of a face of some kind, no doubt a human one. So it's a portrait, or will be, anyway. Not that I can recognize who it's supposed to be—that would be too easy—but it's definitely a face.

I look down at my clothes and am stunned to discover I'm not myself again. That is, I'm not the self of the present: the man now in his fifties, wearing glasses, dressed appropriately for his age. I'm younger, slimmer, wearing a pair of blue jeans, a look I haven't even tried to pull off for a long, long time.

When I walk back into the bathroom and look at my own reflection in the mirror, I'm still not prepared for who I see staring back at me: I'm eighteen again, with a full head of hair and a face as young and innocent as someone even younger. A boy, really. I see my own eyes widen in disbelief and laugh out loud at myself. I didn't notice it at first, but I once again possess the same life force and powerful energy I had at that time—strong muscles, a notable lack of aches or pains, and a self-confidence I'd forgotten I ever had.

Still, it's not all fountain of youth. I'm me, so all the habits of that age come along with me. I find a pack of cigarettes in my shirt pocket, and yes, I was drinking regularly by then… if not daily, then pretty nearly every day. I open the top of the cigarette box and look down to see one of the items next to the four cigarettes inside is a perfectly rolled joint. That figures.

I really don't know what to do. I quit smoking years after this, about a year after I stopped drinking. I don't want to smoke again, not even with an eighteen-year-old body. I'm still me in my mind, and the fifty-something mind still works. I pull out the joint and the scent wafts up with its weird familiarity. Haven't been around that at all for a good twenty-five years, unless I count smelling it at a concert. I put it back into the cigarette pack for now.

With a start, I suddenly realize how I actually *have* matured over these last thirty-plus years. No one's ever accused me of being mature, but I have developed something of a filter.

I don't automatically say what's on my mind, which means I've become a bit more guarded. In those teens and early twenties years, I just let it fly, and damn the consequences. Now I'm more likely to measure out my words slowly—at least, slower than my mind can think them.

I do feel a sense of trepidation about leaving this room behind. I know someone out there is waiting for me, or at least about to encounter me in some way.

Another of your relations, M'Extezuh said. He also said, *Let us go*, but there's no sign he came along for the ride.

I think my sense of trepidation goes along with his absence somehow. I wonder if I'm supposed to go right back into meditation again in search of him, in search of answers. I realize now I don't know where I was before this. Yes, I was with M'Extezuh and The Coordinator in a room, but was it this one? I don't think so. I also don't know whether it even matters. I'm a little lost, regardless of where I go or what I do next. It's all intuitive now, and my intuition has been known to send me both to incredible heights and to unspeakable depths.

The hell with it. I'm going to meditate again on principle.

I go back to the sanctuary meditation, to Kent Falls. It's darker somehow this time. When I call out to M'Extezuh, nothing happens.

I feel distracted. I feel I have to go, even though I do not feel I am ready.

How do you know when it's time to go? How does anyone ever know? I recall with unusual clarity the moment I left Connecticut for good, driving to an unfamiliar place with a rented truck, towing a car. There was a woman there, an ex-girlfriend. We'd reconnected and she came to see me off. Would our romance be rekindled?

It was cold that morning in Connecticut. We kissed goodbye. Everything I owned was packed into that truck. I was off on another adventure, driving to a city where I knew exactly one person, leaping in the hopes that a net would appear. No job awaited me. Yet somehow I knew the time had come.

"I've got to go," I said to the girl, my heart overfull, knowing it was true, not knowing why. And then I drove and drove and drove. That was the last time I saw her.

Now it's like that again, only I'm here *and* there: I'm back in my bed asleep, the Coordinator said, but here I am in my body. My body from when I was younger and stronger, bolder, crazier. My heart overfull, filled with longing and rage, sadness and wonder. I have to go out that door to meet someone in my family, someone I somehow have to comfort.

I can't meditate on this anymore. I have to do it.

I open my eyes.

FOURTEEN

OUTSIDE THE DOOR, IT'S LIKE A RERUN OF THE LAST REEL IN A MOVIE: BRISTOL, CONNECTICUT, AGAIN, RIGHT IN FRONT OF THE OLD BRISTOL BANK & TRUST. Exactly where I landed before I saw my Aunt Jane.

Somehow, though, I sense it's a later era. I start to walk in the same direction as before. The cars around me all fall into that grey area between the distant past and present, and a quick mental calculation tells me if I'm really in my late teens, it's the early 1980s. The vehicles confirm it—most of them look like late 70s models, so that's where I must be.

I walk down Riverside Avenue again, not sure why, exactly. Again, purely intuitive. The past pulls me along like a kite on a string. Should this be easier than I think it will? All I have to do is comfort, not control. I can't change anything. *Not even God can change the past*, I think.

But I don't know who it's going to be. *Another of your relations.* Logic tells me it's got to be someone even closer than Aunt Jane, someone who suffers, or suffered, from alcoholism. That narrows it down to my Dad, his father, or my brother. Or maybe it's another woman.

Who? Someone not as close to me as my aunt? A great-aunt, one of those grandmotherly figures I barely knew? My brain whirls with weird possibilities. The trepidation of not knowing what I'm doing or where I'm going begins to take over again. I try to push it back, walking faster, totally unable to determine the destination.

Then it dawns on me: I can *run*.

I didn't actually start running as a solo activity until after I turned twenty-five. But I'm physically even younger than that now, and the cigarette damage to these eighteen-year-old lungs shouldn't prevent me from running. I pick up speed and move from a brisk walk to a comfortable trot—eyes straight ahead, pacing myself. *This is more like it*, I think. My shoes aren't ideal, but they'll do for now. *I'm only eighteen*, I tell myself, though even this younger version still feels older.

Down the avenue I jog, glancing at trees and buildings as they go by. Then I see it—a low, squat building at 211 Riverside. A laundromat occupies two-thirds of the building, nothing remarkable about it at all. But the right-hand side third of the building is a legendary Bristol dive bar: the Comeback, a.k.a. "Scumback," Lounge.

The Comeback Lounge had a reputation as a biker bar where shitty blues bands could get gigs. It eventually closed, reopened, then closed again multiple times under different management, with different names. It's a place I never entered but heard about from other young fellow travelers, heavy drinkers like my brother, and some of his drinking buddies.

I pull up short and stand outside the building, hands on my knees, panting, looking up at the sign. Could that be it? My own brother?

It could be. He drank like I did, only more so. And if I'm eighteen, he's got to be about twenty-one—a couple years before he got sober. My memories from that period are so dim, so sparse, I might as well have had a lobotomy.

I glance down at my wrist and I'm wearing a watch again, a sports watch this time. It's 4:00 p.m., and even with only three cars in the lot, I know people are drinking inside.

And so I open the door.

The Scumback is what I expected, and the first thing to hit me is the stench—stale cigarettes and beer, along with the odor of fresh cigarette smoke wafting through the air. It's dimly lit, the kind of dive bar you can enter when the sun is blazing but inside it looks like it could be any time. There's an uneven pool table, so shit shots count. I'm instantly sure someone could drink all night here and no one's going to cut him off.

Only four denizens of this dive sit at the bar, which tells me at least one of them walked, or hitchhiked, here. The biker dudes are less a surprise than the lone, slim figure seated away from them. His hair is long, brown, and unnaturally curly. In front of him sit not one, not two, but three different drinks.

I walk up to my brother as if in a dream.

"Hey, man."

"Holy shit." He laughs out loud when he sees me, drags slowly on his cigarette. "You're slumming today, eh? How'd you know I was here?"

I laugh without sound, hoisting myself onto the barstool beside him. "You wouldn't believe me if I told you."

He eyes me with suspicion. "They didn't send you down here to try to haul me back to the ranch?"

Now it's my turn to laugh aloud. "No, man. I'm here of my own volition. I think."

"Here's mud in your eye." He lifts the shot and downs it, then gulps some of the beer as a chaser.

"What are you drinking there?"

He points to each in turn, "Shots of Cuervo, Rumple Minze on the rocks, Stroh's in the bottle."

I nod. "I figured you'd stick with the usual regimen."

"What are you having? I'll get the first round."

I don't know how to respond. Am I supposed to pick up here? My mind hasn't touched a drop in years, even though this eighteen-year-old version of me has…I think.

Then I realize I'm not even sure what body I inhabit. Is it a mirage? Do I only look like me, or am I really back in my past body but with my future mind? I don't know, and it hasn't been an issue until now.

Without even thinking it through I say, "I'm still hung over from last night," but even as the words come out, I know what he'll say next.

"Ah, come on. A little hair of the dog."

I chuckle. "Maybe in a bit."

As we speak, the bartender is already bearing down on us—a biker-type, glowering with disapproval at my boyish

face and the 80s haircut, parted in the middle and feath-
ered back.

"You got ID?"

"I'm just going to have a Coke," I say. If I'm only
eighteen, I'm too young to drink legally here. Already an
alcoholic but too young to drink. The irony is surreal.

"That your brother?" he asks Bob—like I'm invisible, or
too stupid to speak for myself.

"Yep. Chip off the old blockhead, eh?" They both laugh.
I join in, uneasy, not sure what comes next, what I'm even
supposed to say or do.

Bob turns to me. "You've never been here before, huh?"

I shake my head. "Nope. It's not really as bad as people
make it sound." This is probably true at four in the afternoon,
though I suspect I might change my mind by midnight.

"It does the job. Relax, nobody's going to bother us
here. I know all these guys."

I glance around the bar without reassurance. It seems
impossible, yet somehow plausible, that he knows these
guys. They ignore us completely, but I don't feel the sense
of menace I recall from times in later years when I strolled
into other biker bars, like the Coppermine. I sip my Coke.

"This is fucking weird. I don't really know what I'm
doing here," I admit.

"It's fine," he says, dragging on the cigarette again.
"Seriously, you can relax. It's not as fancy as some of the
other bars in town, but they ain't my style anyway."

"No, it's not that," I say. "I mean I'm not sure what I'm
supposed to do next."

He looks at me, bemused. "You mean in this bar or on
this planet?"

"Probably a little of both."

This really cracks him up. "Man," he says, "none of us know. Even the adults are putting on a fucking front. They don't know what they're doing any more than the rest of us."

"Really?"

He taps the ashes off the end of the cigarette into an overflowing ashtray. "Remember when they took us to that Kiss concert? You were what, twelve?"

"Thirteen, I guess."

"Yeah, 'cause I was sixteen. That's right. If you were a parent now, and you had a couple kids in their early- to mid-teens, would you drop them at a concert like that?"

"I don't know. What do you mean?"

"Mike, come on—think about it. Pretty much all their songs are about fucking. They're like, 'Ode to My Cock.' Let's see, you got *Rocket Ride, Plaster Caster. Love Gun.*" He starts laughing again. "Dude named an album after his dick."

I laugh with him. "Jesus, you're right. They're pretty religious, but they never listened to those lyrics. They'd shit."

"*She's* pretty religious. Not him."

"You don't think so?"

"Nah. I've thought for years he's just along for the ride. He'd rather be out in the mountains rock collecting. Being the Old Prospector."

"Holy cripe," I say, a deadpan imitation of the old man.

My brother laughs harder, then erupts into a spasm of smoker's cough. As if it's a segue from the coughing, he says, "Hey, did you quit smoking, too?" He looks at my empty hands sitting in front of the Coke.

"No, I got a few left in this pack." I pull out the cardboard box, shake it open.

His eyes widen a bit when he sees the joint. "Aha, very nice. I gotta get more smokes later. Cigarette machine's broken in here. Gimme one of those for now—and we can save that for later," he adds, indicating the joint with a gesture. "You owe me one."

"What?" I say. "I owe you one? For what?"

"For turning you onto it in the first place." He laughs again, slapping me on the shoulder. Then he grabs the joint out of the box and pockets it, glancing around as if to make sure no one notices it's not a tobacco cigarette. Like any of these guys would care. They're probably all holding. In fact, they've probably got stashes of harder drugs than weed.

"Where do you usually go from here?" I ask, not sure what line I'm pursuing. "You hit the King's Road Inn after this?"

He huffs a little laugh, turns back to the drinks. "No, I'm gonna roll on out to the Pub Café after this place closes down for the night."

"Why?"

He looks over with comic disdain at his uninformed younger sibling. "It's after-hours only, bro."

"There's an after-hours joint in Bristol, Connecticut? What the fuck?"

"Yeah. Special, eh?" We both laugh. "Can you even get into a bar yet down in Virginia?" he asks. "Or you have to wait until your birthday next month?"

This jolts me, as it places us precisely in time: October, 1983. My mind is blown, but I still try to respond right away. "Next month, yeah," I say. "It's nineteen for beer and wine, twenty-one for everything else."

"Weird." He chuckles. "Guess you'll be drinking a lot of beer then. Unless you're planning on getting into Gallo Port."

We make the same face, pure mock horror, and crack up again. It's an inside joke, our mother being the only non-alcoholic in the household. In the early 1980s, she still drinks a tiny glass of port wine before bed—with ice in it, because it's "too strong."

"So," he says, "if you're going to drink anything tonight, we'll have to get the fuck out of here. Why don't we go smoke this thing?"

I now realize there's no way I can hang with my brother and *not* drink or drug. That lifestyle lasted for years for both of us, and it almost killed us. Miraculously, we survived.

Yet I'm still not sure if this eighteen-year-old version of me is really *me*. If I drink or smoke now, am I blowing my current sobriety? Is it like a dream, or real time travel? Up until now, I haven't truly known which. I still don't.

In that moment, I decide it's a freebie. I can do this, and it's in the past. It doesn't count against my sobriety, which started years later. And so I say, "Yeah, man. Let's go."

We walk out into the bright sunlight and I immediately doubt myself again when I see David standing alone on the corner. He looks sad, like he's seen something that disappoints him. Is it me? Us?

Almost at the same exact moment, I realize my brother doesn't see him. In fact, I can guarantee no one else does. David appears as an apparition—not solid like a human, but translucent, like a ghost in a movie.

"Hang on a second," I say. "I got to tie my shoe."

I move closer to the corner, close enough to hear David in the event he should say something to me. Something, anything, to guide me in this situation.

"Why are you going all the way over there to do it?" my brother asks.

"The light's better." An absurd response, a non sequitur. It gets a laugh. I look at David, his child's face, the large, sad eyes. I ask a question with only my own eyes.

He nods sadly, seriously, closing his eyes. And then he fades away, dissolving before me.

What did it mean? Go ahead and do it? Get high?

"Come on, man," my brother says. "We can't torch this fucker up in front of the bar."

And that answers the question. I'm about to get wasted again.

FIFTEEN

 Ritual may not be important for the casual user, but for chronic addicts and alcoholics, at least some small part of the comfort—the warm glow or rush—comes from the ritual around it.

The harder the drug, the more it seems to matter. Heroin or speedball addicts get attached to the works, the needle and spoon, various containers. Cokeheads, in our day, had tiny spoons on chains, tiny glass vials.

With weed, it was all about the bowl or the bong. I flash back in time to my brother telling me about a legendary bowl shaped like a skull that he and his party buddies used. They dubbed it *El Skell*, imbuing it with an almost animal power. I too had a bowl, the end of which was shaped liked a small skull. I remember scraping the sticky black resin out of it and smoking that when I ran out of weed—another, sadder ritual.

But for a joint between brothers, the ritual is stripped back to its bare bones. Two guys, one joint. Take a hit, hold it in, pass the thing back and forth. Don't slobber on it. As basic as it gets.

We stand behind the Scumback building, passing the joint in silence. Big hits, no coughing. Holding the smoke until it almost disappears.

It's been a long time since I've smoked anything, and with restless unease I wonder how it will affect me. I think about our family's history with smoking. I was still a boy when my mother quit cigarettes, but my father smoked his entire life.

While I ponder this, my brother starts talking again. I'm only half paying attention, but he's telling me about some other young guys in town, people I don't know.

"They used to buy a whole bunch of those bumper stickers that say *How's My Driving? Call 1-800-EAT-SHIT*—and they'd go around and find cars or trucks that have the real ones, *Call 1-800-BLAH-BLAH-BLAH*, and they'd put the *EAT SHIT* stickers over the real ones. They did all sorts of stuff like that. Probably got a few people fired with that one."

He laughs and I nod, smiling. It's not really funny to my fifty-something mind, but I understand how the eighteen-year-old version of me must have some appreciation for being an asshole, defacing property for the sole purpose of getting a juvenile laugh at someone else's expense. In my heart somewhere I can still call up that kind of pointless anger, pure testosterone. I remember driving drunk on a dark road at night, throwing an empty beer bottle out the window of the moving car into the woods, hearing it shatter against a tree. A sad sound, savage and brief.

And with that, the heaviness of all this, the sadness, wells up and threatens to overwhelm me. I wonder, if I get tearful, can I play it off as smoke in my eyes? At this juncture my brother surely won't understand why I feel sadness around the drug ritual, sadness about smashing a beer bottle against a tree, sadness at the loss of time and consciousness. I know I can't explain it—not yet, at least.

I don't know what I can or can't explain, or even what I'm here to accomplish. Certainly, smoking a joint wasn't in my plans. Though as we continue to smoke, inhaling and ex-haling, it gradually dawns on me that nothing is happening to me. I don't know why this is so—sometimes first-time pot smokers don't get high at all—but then, I'm not really a first-timer, am I? Or, even more mysterious, maybe it's impossible to lose my sobriety in this state. Maybe I can smoke and drink all night yet remain unaffected. Is that part of the game? Is that my role here as a whizzer, or player, or whatever the hell I am now?

I believe it is. I believe I'm going to be here longer than I'd anticipated. Already I have been back in this early 80s version of my hometown far longer than I spent in New York with Phil Ochs or in Mississippi with Faulkner. Even the adventure into Coleridge's world, with its cold evening walk, didn't last as long.

While I think this, continuing to smoke, I look down and notice a beaten, worn penny on the ground near us. I pick it up and hold it in front of my brother.

He grins with a glimmer of sarcasm as he quotes one of our grandmother's many aphorisms. "*Find a penny, pick it up, and all the day you'll have good luck.*"

"Nah, fuck that." I hurl the penny against the back of the building. It bounces with a small ping into the gutter.

He laughs, then erupts in a spasm of coughing. "Oh, jeez."

"You want to save the rest of that for later?" I gesture toward the roach in his hand, which is almost too hot to hold now.

"Yeah." He licks his finger, then puts the joint out in the saliva mark. I marvel as he calmly puts the roach into his nearly empty cigarette pack, recalling how often we used to do things like that without so much as blinking. In my sober fifty-something mind, it strikes me as bizarre, grotesque, unsanitary. My face must register some of that, as he looks up at me and says, "What?"

"Nothing." I shake my head. "We out of here?"

"Yeah, let's go. You got some kind of fake ID to get into the Pub Café? If not, I can't close this place down, like I was originally planning. I already know they're going to card you here, so—your call."

"Let me see," I say, flipping open my wallet. I don't know what I've got in there, of course. In my real-life teens, I never did own any sort of fake ID.

Bob laughs. "You don't know whether you've got one or not?" He coughs some more. He's definitely high *and* drunk now, so it doesn't occur to him that this is profoundly weird.

To my surprise, I do have a fake ID. His comments have confirmed I'm nineteen, but the ID lists me as twenty-two. Not that big a stretch, though I doubt I look more than seventeen.

"Yeah, man. Here it is." I proffer the card and he examines it with amusement.

"So, you're my age now, huh?" He laughs again. "Guess I can't introduce you as my little brother. How about I say you're my *big* little brother?"

This is another inside joke, as I'm an inch or two taller than him. "I don't care, man. You can introduce me any way you want, or not at all."

"How come you didn't just give that to the bartender in the Comeback?"

"You know me, bro. I can't drink anything alcoholic before I get high, or I'll get sick. You don't want me puking on your leather jacket later."

He pulls another face. "Fuck no. I forgot about that. That little special order you need to do things. But now we've smoked, you can drink all night, eh?"

"Yep. As long as I don't smoke any later. You want that roach tonight, it's gonna be all yours."

"Coolidge. More for me." He laughs again. "Hey, you drove here, right?"

"No, man." I realize I don't have a good excuse for walking or hitching all the way down here, though I suppose he must have a reason of his own—suspended license, DUI, something. I opt for the first thing that pops into my head. "Car broke down, so I walked."

"Fucking American cars. They all suck now, don't they?"

I nod. "We're going to have to start buying Japanese one of these days."

"Let me run back in and see if Big Charlie's going over there. We could ride with him in his truck." He looks over his shoulder to confirm. "He didn't take the Harley today."

"All right." I stand outside the Scumback with the names *Charlie* and *Harley* colliding in my head and realize I later wrote a song that started with those names. Was it from a memory, a dream…or a premonition of this visit to the past?

> *Fat old Charlie with his two-ton Harley was politically incorrect*
> *And black-eyed Phil with his powders and pills was chemically suspect*
> *And poor little Jeanie with her big blue meanies was really quite a wreck*
> *They had one thing in common, they were trying to ease the load*
> *And they were riding down that suicidal road.*

My brother walks back out with Big Charlie, and immediately I recognize him. He's a huge biker dude with a giant beard and a pot belly, all denim and bad tattoos. It hits me that I've never seen him in his drinking days, but will meet him in meetings in the 1990s.

I already know how Charlie's story turns out. It's not good. After a few years of sobriety, at some point he's going to drink again. While he's still in relapse, one of his biker associates will kill a woman, then call on Charlie for help. No longer the master of good judgment, he will help the guy dispose of the woman's body across state lines. When they inevitably track down the murderer, they'll get Charlie, too. They'll charge him as an accessory after the fact and send him to federal prison.

This is a man I only knew sober. I held hands with him while we said the Lord's prayer. Without a doubt, I stand looking at him with infinite sorrow, knowing what's going to happen, the terrible choices he will make, the even more terrible price he will pay. But he doesn't know any of this, doesn't even know me yet.

"What the fuck is your problem?" are his first words to me. "You got something against bikers, college boy?"

My brother comes to the rescue. "He's cool, man, he's cool. Bro, what's going on? Something happen while I was in there? You look like someone stole your lunch money."

I shake my head, trying to shake it all off. "No, man, I was thinking about something. Recent breakup. Sorry, guys."

Big Charlie laughs. "Jesus, boy. I like pussy as much as the next guy, but you've got to let that shit go. You're young, go get some bubblegum on your dick."

We all laugh. In my case, I can laugh mainly because a totally different type of person once said the exact same thing to me. The whole situation here is so surreal, I don't know what to do next.

But of course that's already been decided. We're all heading to the Pub Café in Big Charlie's pickup.

SIXTEEN

THE PUB CAFÉ SITS LIKE AN ABANDONED BOMB SHELTER
AT THE END OF AN EMPTY STREET.

I thought the Comeback Lounge was a dive, but the
Pub Café takes squalor to a whole other level. The stench
assaults the senses as soon as the door swings open, and even
in dim light I can see right away how filthy a dive it is.

Every surface looks sticky—the bar stools, the overflowing ashtrays, the bar itself. Everything I touch somehow
touches me back in a way that makes me shudder. Nor is my
profound disgust exacerbated by smoking weed before riding
over here. I still don't feel any effect, and I suspect I won't feel

anything even when I take a drink. But I know if I somehow actually got stoned and drunk, this place is so vile it would make me vomit.

We sit at the bar in silence, drinking and smoking. I'm almost out of cigarettes and will probably soon be bumming them from my brother's new pack. Big Charlie chain smokes Camel no-filters, swigging bottled Budweiser with grim determination. I picture his demeanor in the future when he's sober, and it now seems almost preposterous. He will become a pretty cool dude once he stops drinking, at least for a time. But I also recall the look in his eyes that remained, even in sobriety—a wildness, like someone who's taken a few too many acid trips.

My brother perches on a barstool between us, though, so there's not likely going to be much conversation over the din of Black Sabbath and Deep Purple from the jukebox. He goes right back to his regimen of Cuervo, Stroh's and Rumple Minze. I order a White Russian, a sweet drink with enough milk in it to settle my stomach in the event that it does somehow fuck me up.

I'm not thrilled with the combined taste of cigarettes, coffee liqueur, milk, and vodka, and for a moment I wonder if the intoxicating effects of alcohol also dulled my taste buds in the bad old days. But I remember how things changed after I stopped drinking and then stopped smoking. People always say, *Things taste better after you quit smoking.* That's not accurate, though. What they really mean is, *You'll taste things better.* In other words, things that taste good will taste great, and things that don't taste good will taste like shit.

I ponder this as I drag on the cigarette and think about what I'm doing here. I still don't know. All along the instruction has been vague but somewhat consistent; you're there to bring comfort, however temporary, to someone.

Now? I don't know. Am I really supposed to do that without warning my brother of future perils, telling him he's an alcoholic…something? Maybe it's Big Charlie I'm supposed to help somehow. After all, my brother and I will be sober *and* free in the future. I already know Big Charlie's heading to prison.

The song on the jukebox ends and the next selection comes on, *Jailbreak* by Thin Lizzy. Is that a sign for me, an instruction to bring comfort to Big Charlie? And how? The guy is a sociopath at this point, and I'm not even sitting next to him, much less able to come up with words of comfort. *Hey, Charlie, don't worry. It's okay. You're going to go to prison and whatnot, but I guess you won't die right away. I don't know.*

Where's the Coordinator when I actually need him? David? M'Extezuh?

As if in answer to the questions in my mind, I look toward the dim corner of the bar near the door and suddenly see David. I'm sure he wasn't standing there last time I looked.

He is dressed in completely different clothes than when I saw him outside the Scumback only a short while ago. He's solid again, not some sort of translucent apparition. But he still looks infinitely sad, his eyes boring into me with that unsettling wisdom and dignity far beyond his years.

"I got to take a leak," I tell the guys, pretending to head for the restroom. Instead, I circle around the bar towards David, hoping to get guidance or direction on what I'm supposed to do.

As I get closer, though, I freeze in mid-step. David holds his hands out and open in a gesture like a statue of

Jesus or Mary. That's what brings me to a halt. I feel certain he's really here, engaged somehow with what's going on, but maybe he's not able to advise or admonish. And at the moment I think this, he slowly shakes his head *no*, and turns translucent, dissolves, disappears. I'm alone again in the middle of a dive bar.

Now I wonder more than ever why I'm here. Am I in a dream? I remember something David said to me early on—*Sometimes I sleep through the night like normal kids, but mostly I go on these little excursions*—and I think I know what's happened here.

I'm dreaming all this. It's always been nothing but a stupid dream. I could kill or steal or commit any kind of crime, and it wouldn't matter. It didn't really happen.

That's why I'm not high from the joint or drunk from the White Russian. Over the years in sobriety, I've had dreams where I'm drunk—and not only drunk, but aware in the dream that I'm in relapse, and have been for quite some time. Yet I cannot recall the feeling of drunkenness in the actual dream itself. I wake from these drunk dreams in a fever pitch of anxiety, afraid I've blown my sobriety. Then I have to think hard before I realize no, it was all a dream, I wasn't in relapse before or during the dream. A terrible game the brain plays on alcoholics, even when sleeping, even after years of recovery.

So I'm not drunk, I'm not high. I'm in a dream. A stupid one, at that. All this bullshit with David and some mythical Coordinator figure, and some made-up spiritual guide I created, is all just that: bullshit. I could walk up to that dream version of Big Charlie and punch him right in the fucking face, and it wouldn't make a difference.

He can't hurt me. I'm asleep.

But okay, I'll play along. After all, it's an especially vivid, convincingly realistic dream, and mostly within the bounds of conventional reality, other than the gigantic cockroach and the time travel. Sure, I'll pretend it's still real. I'll make some decisions, too. I'll go back to that bar and talk to my brother. Tell him what's what.

"Hey, man."

"That was fast," he says. "No line in the latrine?"

I laugh. "No. Besides, I kind of wanted to get back here to tell you something."

He sips his Rumple Minze on the rocks. "What's that?"

"This—" I gesture around us, encompassing the bar, Big Charlie, everything, "—it's all bullshit."

"I know that," he says, to my surprise. "You think I don't know that?"

I have to stop and think what to say. What does the dream version of me tell the dream version of my brother? Nothing? Everything? Something in between?

"I mean the drinking thing," I say before I can stop myself. "I mean the drinking and the drugs. We're both committing suicide, very slowly and inefficiently. The good news is we're both going to get sober. You're probably going to go through another rehab or two, but you'll come out the other side and never drink again. I'm actually in my fifties now, and—"

SEVENTEEN

WHEN I AWAKE—MERE MOMENTS LATER, IT SEEMS—I FIND MYSELF AT THE TOP OF A HILL. A cool wind blows down across the bright grey trees, which hold no leaves. In an instant I know it's autumn, it's still Bristol, close to the Barnes Nature Center. It's Pigeon Hill, a nickname for a hill at the far end of a seventy acre nature reserve where my brother and I played with our dog when we were kids, camped out with our father under the stars. It's one of the only places in the universe where I ever truly feel at home.

No one here but me. No David, no mystical men. I don't know what's happened, but I can't help thinking somehow I was wrong. It isn't all a dream. It's real. It seems more real than ever.

And so I begin to walk along the trail that winds across the top of the hill. It's like a small mountain, tree-covered, with an occasional boulder. There's one section, up ahead, where I can sit on a couple of shelf-like grey boulders that form a kind of natural chair. Water pools up in some of the indentations, the last leaves of summer scattered around them like lonely children.

I sit for a few moments to get my bearings. The sound of the wind comforts me. I look across the spaces between the trees to where I can just make out a few unnatural colors—houses, one of which was ours throughout my childhood and a few years beyond, until my parents' inevitable divorce. I strain to see the shapes of the houses, but the trees obscure them too much. I can't tell which is ours.

Then I hear the sound of walking. It sounds like it's coming my way. I don't want to see anyone now. I can't bear the thought of having to make small talk with a stranger, some version of *how you doing*, obligatory and hollow.

But I won't have to worry about that. It's the Coordinator and M'Extezuh, coming over the rise.

I can't believe this, yet a part of me can. Somehow they have to be here, and I do too. I realize for the first time they're not any more in control of the situation than me. I'm a kind of assignment, a problem for them. Someone or something, a higher force or presence, compels them to act…and they have to act upon me.

And because I am so tired—tired and anxious, and still not even sure what I'm supposed to be doing, but knowing I don't want to be doing any of this—I see them almost as if they were enemies.

I stand again, squared up as they approach. I do not wait for either of them to speak first.

"Now what? More punishment? More subterfuge? You think I have to jump through some more spiritual hoops for you?"

They come up to me, exchanging a knowing glance.

"Of course you are angry," says M'Extezuh. "Before you even finished your assignment with your brother, you began to speak to him. You began—"

"Yeah, I began to speak to him. He's my *brother*. You know what? Fuck this. Fuck you both." I wheel on one foot, storming across the hill away from them. Shaking with rage. Panting as I walk faster and faster.

The entire time, I expect something to happen. Waiting for a loud voice of censure, something stopping me, some force freezing me in my tracks.

Nothing happens. They do not follow. I walk until I reach the crest of the hill and look out across the sandpits, where distant trees tower over tiny houses in a subdivision that wasn't even built when I last walked here.

When I finally look behind me, I see I'm alone. They didn't follow, didn't stop me. They're gone.

For the first time since the Dweller, I feel truly afraid. At the first bar, at the second bar, even waking up here on this hill, I could convince myself someone or something else was in control. I had a purpose of some sort, though it was obscure to me, something I could only strain after without necessarily knowing. And, most of all, there was certainly an end point to it—or so I thought—an end point to Ochs, to Faulkner, to Coleridge.

Did I push it too far? I was in some kind of grey area with my Aunt Jane, and there were going to be "consequences." I was never too clear on what those were. Then the next thing I knew, I was meeting with my brother, and I pushed it again. I pushed it all the way to the limit. Didn't I?

Now I'm alone again. At some point it will be dark here, and it will get colder. I have no money on me, no car here, no job. Nothing but the clothes on my back.

Am I still in a dream state? Some kind of desolate purgatory? And how do I get back? Where do I even go? My ancestral home?

I decide that's what I have to do. Go back to the home I grew up in. The house, that is. No longer my home. These woods are now, truly, more home to me.

And so I walk. I head down the hill, walking a path I walked so many times when I was ten, eleven, twelve. It winds through the woods, across small wooden bridges over streams, up and down more hills. It's not even a long hike—it was only ever so for a child. For the man, it's almost nothing.

Yet when I emerge from the woods at the end of the trail, looking out onto the field across the street from the house I lived in so many years ago, my heart fills with dread. Am I supposed to approach that door? I don't know the people who live there. What do I say?

Hi. Sorry to bother you. I grew up in this house. Mind if I look around?

Oh, by the way, what year is this? Am I still in the 1980s?

I slow my pace as I pass the Barnes Nature Center building and begin to walk up the road beyond it. As I look for clues to the time, I am struck by the oddity that there are no cars. Nothing to give me a single hint. No children. No sounds of people in any of the houses or yards. It's like the entire neighborhood emptied in anticipation of my arrival. I'm a ghost in my own hometown—a spirit, a shadow.

I slow walk the last few hundred feet to the house. There's nothing for it. I have to get to the front door. Have to knock.

I stand before the front door, waiting. For what?

Nothing. The whole street is silent. Only the faint sound of the wind.

I think of my father and brother and me, camping out beneath the stars on Pigeon Hill in sleeping bags. We must have seen a hundred meteorites that night. My father called them shooting stars.

I remember him, my father, a man with steely thin fingers and calloused fingertips, reaching into my mouth to extract a loose tooth when I was eight years old—the nicotine-stained hand bitter in my mouth like the sap of some poisonous root. He was trying to help me, I knew, the loose tooth driving me to distraction but still hanging by nerves like thick strings, and I not strong enough to tear it free, tears forming in the corners of my eyes from that bitter taste, more overpowering than my own yellowed hand would ever be when, later on, I too smoked a pack or more each day.

All this passes through my mind as I stand at that front door.

I knock.

Silence. Nothingness. There's no one home.

And so I turn and walk back down through the Nature Center parking lot, back into the woods. Back through the trails, across the wooden bridges over the streams, up the hill to the grey shelf-like rocks. I sit back down in the shadows, my back against a shelf of stone. And the wind blows, quiet, gentle, almost like the music of my mind.

EIGHTEEN

HIGH ATOP PIGEON HILL I SIT. It's a curious name, strangely prosaic and not especially appropriate. In all my years growing up in Bristol, I never once saw a pigeon in this area.

I shouldn't be here, I tell myself. *I should go. It's going to be night soon.*

Isn't it?

But the fact is, I don't know. I don't know if I'm really here, in an eighteen-year-old version of myself, having any or all of this experience. Sure, it all seems real. Faulkner, Coleridge, my Aunt Jane. Big Charlie. But David—he didn't seem as real the last couple times I saw him, did he? Never said a word. Never smiled or frowned. Simply shook his head yes or no and dissolved. Faded to black, like a ghost in a movie. Like an illusion.

He was my guide, and now I'm alone. Is that it? Do I even have that right?

As if the thought of David jogs my memory toward some rudimentary understanding of what's happening, I recall the Coordinator's words: *You will have to content yourself at first with following David, then David will have to content himself with following you.*

But then he changed it. *Because of what you've done, you will have to follow David again. Call it a demotion,* he said.

David isn't here, though. Neither are my brother, Charlie, the Coordinator. M'Extezuh. Only me, alone on this hill. It will be dark soon. A light breeze picks up leaves and scatters them around me. I lean back against the shelf-like surface of stone.

I know what I have to do, and I hate it. I hate knowing, and hate doing it even more, because it reveals to me for the hundredth, the thousandth time, how little control I have over anything in this universe beyond my own thoughts and actions.

I have to surrender. I have to let go.

Control—an illusion. Security—illusion. Even danger, really—another illusion.

Here I sit on this rock, connected to an even bigger rock I can't even see, hurtling through space. A hundred years from now, I'll be gone. Hell, probably fifty years from now. The idea that I have any kind of security or control is ridiculous. The one thing I can truly cling to, the one thing I can be secure in, is the knowledge that I am going to die, David is going to die, my brother and wife and friends and neighbors, and everyone I've ever known—every single one of us will be gone someday. Maybe we'll be in some other region, some world of Coordinators and M'Extezuh and Houdini and Nietzsche, but beyond that, there's nothing to hang on to, nothing to prove or deny.

And something primeval or instinctual or defiant in me—something so strong, it's probably stronger than me— rebels with every fiber of my being against this knowledge and its inevitable consequences. When the world is going to hell, and I don't know my next move, the direction I should go, or even my own motives, the one thing I can't bear to even consider doing is to simply present myself to the universe and say, *Here I am. Do with me what you will.*

Yet that's exactly what I must do, isn't it? Even as I think it, I know it's true. The hardest thing for me to do. Let it all go.

I decide to try. I change my position, tuck my legs into a cross-legged meditation position of sorts—uncomfortable on my shelf of stone, to be sure. And I try to meditate with the sound of the wind and the sense that leaves still fly by me here on this hill, in this strange time and place, this being but not-being, knowing but not-knowing. I will meditate at least a little while. I will try to let go. Maybe I will even pray for the willingness to be able to let go. To let go of something, if not of everything. To let go of whatever I can.

Time passes, no idea how much or how little. What does it matter? Minutes or hours, I'm alone, I have no plans or re- sources. I only surrender because I don't have another choice.

After half an hour or hour, maybe more, I hear some- thing different from the sound of the wind blowing, and the little ticking sounds in the distance of the forest. It's a small, rhythmic noise, a tiny crunching that sounds like it could be footsteps coming my way. Small feet, a small person, maybe, like a petite woman or a child.

A child. Of course.

And when I finally open my eyes and look up, I see David strolling over the crest of the hill, with the easy but deliberate swing only a six-year-old could manage. He touches trees absently as he walks, as if saying hello to old friends.

As I watch him, I see that he sees me, and now I know: he already knew I was here, and he's on his way to me. He's my helper, if not my actual salvation. If I am a problem or an assignment for the Coordinator and M'Extezuh, for David I am probably a vocation. I feel myself flush slightly with the knowledge that my six-year-old cousin must care for me like a parent cares for a child.

"Hi, Cousin Mike," he says without anger or even judgment.

"Thanks for coming," I say, not really knowing what else to say. "What's happening? You have to clean up my mess again somehow?"

He shrugs. "It's okay. I make mistakes all the time, too. But I think I get in a little less trouble for mine."

I laugh my sheepish laugh and he smiles. He's so at ease with all this, and has been from the beginning, I can't help but wonder whether we really are dreaming. But no—it's too real. I was kidding myself to ever think it.

David stands before me, while I still haven't moved from the rock. Without sitting down to rest he says, "Let's go."

I get up. "Where are we going?"

"I don't know," he admits. I begin to walk beside him, surprised by the answer if not by its candor.

"Really? We're just going to walk?"

"Yeah, I don't know where we're supposed to go. I know some things, but not everything." He smiles up at me, and the slightly mischievous look returns to his eyes. "You grew up around here."

"I did. This was my playground back in the day, when I was about your age. My brother and me. We'd take the dog down here to the Nature Center, run around on this hill." I hook a thumb over my shoulder, pointing behind us. "We used to run down those sandpits back there. A little dangerous, but nothing crazy."

"And you and your brother camped out with your Dad there, too, right?"

I glance down at him. "Yeah. We packed up sleeping bags and hiked down through the trail, up the hill, and over to the sandpits. We didn't even have a tent. We slept under the stars."

"How was that?"

"It was amazing. In those days, there weren't nearly as many houses or lights around here. We could see so many stars in the night sky. That night, I think I saw more shooting stars than I have the entire rest of my life since."

He nods. "Pretty cool. You're not surprised I know about that?"

"Not really, no."

"Why not, right? If I know about your adventures in Binghamton...."

"You can call them misadventures if you want," I say. "There's a new vocabulary word for you."

He laughs. "I like it. *Misadventures.* Do you think we're going to have some of those while we're out walking?"

"I don't know," I say. "I have to admit, I kind of hope there's a little less drama, not more drama. You really don't know where we're going?"

"Nope. I didn't get any instructions for this at all. I can feel something about it, though, and I know that feeling is true."

"What do you mean?"

He answers the question with a question of his own. "You know how sometimes, when you're out walking and talking with someone, you lose track of your surroundings? You get really into what you're talking about, and you're just in it, and then you realize time has gone by, but you weren't aware of anything around you at all?"

"Yeah, I've had that. Only with a deep conversation with someone, though. I don't think it ever happens to me when I'm walking or running alone."

"No," he says. "It won't."

"How do you know that?"

We continue walking in silence, as if he's thinking about it. "I don't know how I know," he says at length. "I just know."

I nod silently, thinking. Does that mean we need to keep talking in order to get to that place?

"Yes," David says, answering the question I haven't yet said aloud. "It means we need to keep talking in order to get to that place."

I laugh. "Not so sure I like it when you do that."

David laughs along with me. "Try not to teach me any bad words when you're thinking, okay?"

And then he does his little spritely thing, as I like to call it—laughing and dancing and skipping away wildly, like any six-year-old would do. Like any normal kid without a day job, or night job, if that's what this is.

As we walk and talk, I'm still keenly aware of our surroundings for a simple, practical reason: it's a trail through the woods, and I only know one way straight back to my childhood home. But long ago, trailblazers marked the trees on this trail different colors, and we have hiked the opposite direction from the one I would have taken back to the house. The sky-blue marks on the occasional oak or maple tell me we are on the Blue Trail. I only know it goes far out into the woods beyond Bristol, into Whigville or Burlington, somewhere unfamiliar.

"You know where you're going?"

"Not really," says David. "I know the other direction leads back to the road, and it's all familiar territory for you. In order for us—for you—to lose track of your surroundings, we'll have to keep going and going. Far out into the woods, along the trail you don't know as well."

"It's a trail I don't know at all," I admit. "I've been on it once or twice, but I don't remember it. I don't remember if I got lost, or was with a group, or what."

"Some of both," he says. "One time you got lost. The other, you were with a guided group, so there was no chance to get lost."

I shake my head. "I can't believe you know all this stuff about me. I don't remember at all. How old was I then? Do you know that?"

He squints as if to see, and I realize that the woods are already dropping away, as if we are anywhere—a realization that brings them back into focus with distressing clarity. "I think you were about my age when you did the guided group. The getting lost hike came later."

"I never did have the greatest sense of direction."

He laughs, striding ahead with purpose. "Don't worry. We're not going to get lost, because at a certain point, we'll be so in it that we won't even notice anything around us—and when that happens, we're going to end up someplace else."

"You mean disappear and reappear somewhere else like we have before? Doesn't that scare you?"

"No," he says, "that's the fun part."

NINETEEN

WE WALK AND WALK AND WALK, PAST TREES WITH
THEIR PALE BLUE BLAZES, AND AS THEY ZIP PAST US, WE
TALK. Somehow the blur of trees and rocks and leaves becomes more dreamlike, less real, and something changes. I
don't know what it is—we haven't dropped into any different
kind of reality, as far as I can see—but I feel the difference.

"Are we still on the Blue Trail?" I ask.

"I don't know," says David. "Are we? I don't think it
makes any difference."

Now I'm sure it's not the same trail. I sense that everything else is the same—the fecund smell of the dead leaves

and earth and moss beneath them, the green and brown of the leaves, the grey rocks and stones—but something has shifted. We must have reached a point where neither of us were aware of our surroundings, and now we are somewhere else.

Where?

"How do you mean?" I ask. "Wouldn't it make a difference if we're no longer in Connecticut? Or no longer in the 1980s?"

"It's all the same to me," he says, striding forward with his child's pace. "Same adventure, different day."

Now I am fully present again, noticing every crack and crevice, every leaf and branch standing out in sharp contrast to the sky. If I need to lose track of my senses, to let go more, I'm certainly not doing it now.

Then I see it: the next blazed tree, a dollop of paint at eye level on the trunk, and it's not blue. It's not even close. It's a pale yellow mark. Either we are no longer in that time and place, or we have strayed far from the trail, taken a wrong turn somewhere. We're lost.

"Don't worry, Cousin Mike," he says, again reading my thoughts. "We're almost there."

"Where?" I ask. "I don't think we're in Connecticut *or* the twentieth century anymore."

"Still not sure where we are," he says, "but I'm sure we're almost at the end of the line."

A chill runs up my arms at those words. "What do you mean, *the end of the line?*"

"God knows."

"God?"

"Sure," says David. "You believe in God. Higher Power. Whatever you call it. You'll know what you mean when you experience it. Remember what the Coordinator said to you about following? First he said I would follow you, but then he said you have to follow me again."

"Yes," I say. Even with his child's pace, unable to walk as fast as me, there's no question who is leading the way. I walk beside him but I know I'm not the leader here.

"So you walk beside me, but somehow you're following me," David says. "You don't know where we're going."

"No, I don't. But neither do you?"

"Neither do I. Like I said, that's the fun. It's like that expression adults use sometimes, *leap and the net will appear.* Only this is with walking, not jumping."

And as if a door swings open, some kind of portal unlocked by the word *leap*, we come with an abrupt halt to the end of the line. The woods open out in dramatic fashion, not into a clearing, but into what I can only describe as the edge of a cliff. The trees are all behind us, not around us, the space before us wide open. Below lie craggy surfaces, boulders, stumps of trees, and above spreads an open, ominous sky. It would be a long way down—a fatal fall, if we didn't stop in our tracks, if we were alive in the traditional sense and walked right off the edge. Or leapt, hoping for a net.

We stand in place—panting, chests heaving. We have been walking fast for some time, longer than I know or care to measure. I wipe sweat from my brow.

"So, what? We're stuck here? We just wait?"

"I still don't know," David says. "Your guess is as good as mine. Maybe not quite as good, but pretty close." He laughs a little, still panting.

I look around again, getting the lay of the land. The trees behind us waver a bit in the wind close to the edge of the cliff, and I see exactly one tree with a yellow blaze mark on it. If this is the end of the line, that tree and the path beside it must be the beginning.

When I turn around to look back out across the space ahead, the sky cracks open. That is not exactly right, but I have no other words for it. It is as if the world is split apart, but not in a way that feels scary or bad. In a flash my mind returns to the Dweller on the Threshold, because what engulfs me now is the exact opposite of that experience in every way.

When that happened, and I faced my greatest fear, the air around me filled with a terrible whirring sound, the wings of the beast. Now it seems every particle of air around me, and even within me, is filled with the most peaceful, joyous hum I have ever heard or felt in my life—as if a great tuning fork has been struck and the hum runs around and through all creation in one steady and vibrant note.

Aum.

On and on it goes, while I stand rooted to the spot with David. In any other scenario like this, where I feel no ability to move or talk, I would have a profound desire to somehow shield or protect David from whatever force we faced. But in the moment, feeling and hearing this profound and wondrous sound, I know only that there's no need for fear or anger or even sadness. There is nothing to be protected from. This joyous, steady, perfect note enveloping us, and everything around us, can only be one thing.

Pure love.

At length, I sense a shift in my own consciousness, and it feels slightly like when I returned to myself after being unaware of my surroundings, when we were hiking through the woods. The great hum continues, we stand still rooted to the spot, not moving or making a sound, yet something is ever so slightly different.

And then I know what it is.

It's not me. It's my realization that on the other side of the great gulf between us, I can see two figures standing side by side at the edge of their own cliff, their own end of the line. I half expect them to walk on air across to us, but they only stand and beckon.

M'Extezuh and the Coordinator.

Jump.

I cannot at first comprehend what I've heard. Perversely, I think of a bad movie, where a lone figure stands atop a skyscraper, and some inexplicably cruel stranger below yells up to them.

Jump.

I look down to David at the same moment he looks up to me. Does he look up to me? Or does he lead me? I'm the adult here. Are we taking our lives in our hands, or are we taking a literal leap of faith?

Without a word, he reaches up and takes my hand, his eyes never leaving mine. Without a word, he turns back toward the great space beyond, his face beatific in that supreme moment of love and faith. And with that, any fear or hesitation vanishes.

And we jump, hurtling into the space before us.

TWENTY

THE NEXT MOMENTS RUN INTO HOURS. They happen in a realm I can neither understand nor competently describe. All I can do is record impressions.

David and I instantly separate in midair. It turns out that's all right. In an instant we have transformed into some kind of warriors, outfitted for battle like knights from a future epoch.

We can fly, but it feels so much more real than the floaty, vacuum-like atmosphere of all my previous dreams—the out-of-body experiences, as the Coordinator told me.

We swoop and dip and rush into updrafts like birds. Everything happening below and around us is beyond my powers of description. There's a kind of arena so impossibly large, so hard to comprehend, it stretches out for what look like miles. My earthbound mind tells me we hover above a massive stadium, bigger than anything in the so-called real world by a factor of seven or ten or God knows what.

God knows. David's words ring again in my ears as I plummet into the battle below.

And like the arena far beneath it all, this wild airborne battle defies description. To call it *epic* would be an understatement. The sky swarms with warriors of so many types that I cannot even begin to determine who and what they all might be.

Yet I already know what some of them are. I deduce that we have somehow ascended into another level of existence, with hundreds of thousands of souls flying all around us. Some are mere mortals like David and me, some are Coordinators, and some are the next level above "middle management," as David's Coordinator described himself. They are Kings of Coordinators. I cannot say how I even know this from their size and their more ornate golden robes alone. I just *know*.

Flying above this infinite arena, the Kings of Coordinators, the lesser Coordinators, and the mortals like David and me, all engage in battle with some kind of evil spirits. Again, I do not know what they are or what to call these heavier, sinister spirits. But I recognize it is a battle of their forces against ours.

David swoops back up past me and above me, a child in a warrior battle costume, like he is only playing. Is he? Is he a pawn in this game, or actually safe? Is there such a thing, after all? I don't know that either.

"Come on, Cousin Mike," he calls, laughing. Laughing, in the midst of a war. I can only shake my head in disbelief, follow him in hopes that I can somehow lead, somehow protect him from whatever real danger lies here. Surely this is not merely a game, or a dream.

As that thought forms, the scene below drops away. I soar alone into an updraft that takes me so far above the battle that I am suddenly observer, not participant. No sword fight, no sinister enemy. I realize before I can even consider it that I am back near the edge of the cliff.

Somehow I have retreated, or been brought back to solid ground.

I float gently down to the earth, landing in what must be the same spot where we jumped. I look behind me and there stands the tree with the pale yellow blaze. I'm alone here, and David still whoops and hollers somewhere far below me. Do I jump into the void again? Did I retreat under my own power, or has some force guided me back here?

Before I have a chance to wonder further, I see another figure rising to meet me. I know instantly this is a King of Co-ordinators, or whatever they call themselves. His long, flowing golden robe bears swatches ornately decorated with symbols in other colors. He floats above me before landing without sound about ten feet away—facing me, expressionless.

"You are the one I have been hearing so much about," he says.

His tone betrays nothing to indicate whether that's a good or bad thing, but I can't help thinking it's probably not good.

What am I supposed to say? I have no idea but, with my unerring gift for resisting authority, I only reply, "Have you?"

I don't expect a particular response, but one thing I definitely do not anticipate is what happens next: the tall, imposing figure with his longish hair and the stern, aloof bearing of a sovereign throws his head back and laughs.

"My, my," he says when he finishes laughing. "Yes, you are full of the most remarkable unwarranted confidence. I'd heard, but scarcely believed it. You know something of who, or what, I am?"

I smile but stand straight, holding my ground. "I'm not sure how I know it, but I have an intuition you are a king of some kind. Your position elevates you above other Coordinators."

"Yes, that is accurate. I am a King of Coordinators. There are several of us."

"Exactly what I called you in my mind, though I can't say why. Is that an original thought of mine, or have I somehow been granted this knowledge?"

The King nods a couple of times as if in reply. "That can only come from your spirit guide, M'Extezuh. Do you know who M'Extezuh is?"

"I think of him as my spirit guide. David referred to him as a wizard."

"Of course. But you must understand, David is only six years old. As advanced as he is, surely you have noticed he does not have the language to describe everything he experiences."

I nod, then ask, "You mean describe in adult terms?"

"Precisely. He has seen movies, so *wizard* is a term he uses to explain. M'Extezuh has had many incarnations. In the temporal world you normally experience, he was known in his last incarnation as Swami Sri Yukteswar."

Now I know I was right. When I met M'Extezuh in my meditations years ago, I only felt I was in touch with a higher being. A person who has advanced spiritually, like a guru, who can wander around in the spirit world. But I never had the arrogance to think he was someone known to the world—for all practical purposes, famous.

"So my spirit guide is a guru."

"A well-known one, in fact, since you know the name. Why do you suppose you call him *M'Extezuh*?"

"I have no idea. The name came to me, so I've always presumed it's his name."

"Say it again. *M'Extezuh*. What does it sound like?"

I say the name aloud, slowly. "I don't get it. What?"

"In your language, it sounds rather like *My Ecstasy*, does it not?"

The revelation hits me like a thunderbolt. I say it again, aloud, "M'Extezuh." It does sound like it, the way I would say *My Ecstasy* if I were drunk. If I were on the verge of blacking out.

Overwhelmed with emotions I can scarcely identify— gratitude, wonder, confusion—I ask the only thing I can, not knowing whether the King even knows. "But—why?"

He smiles again. "I suspect it has something to do with your ability to experience pleasure. You looked for spiritual answers for years, did you not?"

"Yes, I did," I say. "But I didn't find M'Extezuh until after I found a spiritual solution. Until I found sobriety."

"Indeed," the King says. "And without knowing, then, in finding him, you'd found your ecstasy. Your joy."

I hug my arms tight across my chest. I'm well aware it's a defensive posture, but I can't say for sure what I am defending myself from, or why. "Do you know why I walked away from it? That is, why I stopped meditating so regularly and deeply, why I stopped seeking M'Extezuh out?"

"Yes, I think I do," he says. "For that most natural of all reasons for men: you like sex."

I laugh hard, so abruptly I almost choke. Then I laugh harder, until the tears stream down my cheeks. "That's it. You're right. I got so far into meditation, into studying it, feeling like I was in touch with a Higher Power, I was afraid I'd have to take the next logical step in that direction and become a monk. But I love women, and I wanted to see whether I could marry and start a family."

Now the King folds his arms as well, looking at me with kindness but also with a kind of paternal seriousness. "I don't know that it was so much the women themselves you loved, though. It was the sex, or simply the possibility of sex."

I cannot deny it, and in a flash I see my history in relationships—like someone's life passing before his eyes, only in this case, his love life.

I smile ruefully. "Yes," I say. "Yes, I suppose that is so. Looking for ecstasy there, not in the spiritual world."

"Now you understand more," the King says.

"Was I wrong after all? Should I have tried to be celibate, to become a monk?"

The King laughs again, a deep chuckle. "No, you would never have succeeded. You know better than that."

"I suppose so. Though I already had the hair for it," I say, indicating the large bald spot and the fringe of hair around it.

"You've practiced that one a few times, haven't you?" he asks, still smiling. "Come, you don't have to play court jester for a King of Coordinators."

For the first time I look down, abashed. "You're right, of course. I'm still somewhat lacking in humility, even after all this time."

"You're better off now than you were when you first learned the difference between humility and humiliation, though."

I don't know whether he's going to continue or if I should speak again. Without waiting for much of a pause, I ask, "What am I doing here, Your Highness—assuming that's what I should call you?"

"This assignment should be much more than you following David around, or David following you. I am certain you understand this much."

"Yes."

"You have been granted a gift given only to a few—you are doing, right now, something that took years of practice and discipline for Sri Yukteswar."

"What's that?"

He laughs again, silently. "Remember what the Coordinator told you? You are in two places at once. Only with years of yoga study did Sri Yukteswar gain the ability to do this in real time—conscious, though not to any great purpose. It was merely part of his effort to attain a higher level of spiritual development, and to show others it was possible to do so."

"And me? I'm doing that now?"

"Yes, but only in your sleep. Again, not to any great purpose back in the temporal world, where you are more or less unconscious. The difference is that Sri Yukteswar strove for years after this. You, on the other hand, fell into it the way a chimpanzee falls asleep."

Now I laugh. "I feel like I should be a little insulted here. But I'm also sure you're right. Why did I receive such a gift?"

"You made a comment not long ago—a derogatory one, you'll recall—about a sort of cosmic pecking order. You know of what I speak?"

I blush, in spite of myself. "Yes, I remember. I was angry."

"Indeed," he says. "The restraint of tongue only comes to you occasionally when your emotions run high. Still, you were essentially correct. Above the Coordinators are those like myself, Kings of Coordinators. But there are levels above Kings as well."

"So you're saying, you don't know?"

"I am saying I don't know. Presumably, there is a reason. May you remain, or at least become, worthy of the gift."

"May I presume to ask another question?"

He looks at me. "Yes."

"This gift of being in two places at once—am I to do something with it back there? I mean, back at home, where I'm sleeping even now?"

"Yes," he says. "But not yet. Only when you return. For now, there is something more you must do."

TWENTY ONE

In my mind, I flash back to a time years ago, and the image strikes me with peculiar clarity—the dismal boarding house where I lived when I was newly sober, the shattering acid flashback with its neon cockroaches skittering across the dirty ceiling. Then, further back in the recesses of my mind, the original bad trip: bloody slashes like knife wounds leaping out from a whirl of furiously moving geometric patterns.

That night went on for days, it seemed, when I lay alone on my bed, paralyzed by the horror of it all, staring awestruck at the ceiling. In a way more real than surreal, I felt I stood on a ledge and looked down. It was the ledge of my own sanity. I looked and looked, not jumping, but not deciding not to, either. I froze, but I made a decision not to make a decision.

At length, the patterns shifted and receded, and I was back. Closer to sanity—forever changed, if not ruined.

All this ricochets around my head in a matter of moments as I look down on the battle scene below. I have no weapon, yet somehow am still arrayed in this futuristic warrior's uniform.

And so I close my eyes and leap into the void again.

TWENTY TWO

 I'm dressed for battle, ready to fight side by side with David against whatever dark forces we're supposed to conquer.

I think I know all this because the King of Coordinators told me right before I jumped that I had to face my greatest test of all. Yet when I jump, I feel no fear; only elation.

By now I understand what will typically happen. In the blink of an eye, I'm somewhere else. It's disorienting, but I'm used to it. So when I open my eyes again, I should be ready for anything.

But this time I blink awake to the exact opposite of anything I expect. Somehow, in the midst of all the drama, I think my leap will be back into the fray, David by my side. Instead, I find myself in a bright, quiet room.

Everything is white and grey, and at first, I don't understand what's happened or where I am. When I blink a few more times, the veil lifts and my awareness levels back up to normal—to high alert, even. I hear distant sounds down an adjacent hallway, and it only takes another second to realize that I am in a hospital.

I almost panic right here. Am I back in the Children's Cancer Center? I can't bear to see children sick or dying. But when I look down to my right, I see I'm in a chair and David sits beside me in a smaller, child-sized chair. He's looking straight ahead, smiling.

"David. Thank God you're here. Where are we?"

He looks up at me, still smiling, then turns his gaze straight ahead again and nods. The smile fades, and I look to where he's looking, down the long angled hallway. I see only the left-hand edge of a doorway and a sliver of the room from this vantage point.

"Please tell me it's not another dying child," I say. "I can't handle that kind of thing."

"No," says David. "He's not dying. Come on." He takes my hand, and I feel the power it gives me as I am able to stand and walk forward—reluctantly, but still capable of movement.

As we walk down the hallway, I feel a strange familiarity about the place come over me. Is it something I've dreamed?

A hospital where I visited someone who was sick? I try to avoid these places as much as I can, but I've been known to visit a friend after surgery. This doesn't look like something recent, though. The feel of it all is late sixties, early seventies. The machinery looks outdated, almost like something from a movie I saw a long time ago.

And then I know. Everything slows down, like in the moments of an accident or a major injury. A nurse walks toward us, a young freckle-faced woman with longish brown hair and a name tag that says *Lynn* on it. She gives us the perfunctory smile of the young nurse greeting a male visitor, not the same warm smile that shone down on the little boy in the bed with the fractured skull.

"It's me," is all I can say. "I'm going to meet myself." Still walking, still feeling like someone caught in a strange, surreal dream.

"Yes," David says. "You remember what I told you before? When you were in this hospital, a boy my own age, you got this feeling of safety, of warmth and peace?"

"I remember. You told me it was a whizzer."

"That's right," he says. "Let's go in and say hi. Visiting hours are almost over."

Still in the strange, dreamlike state, I walk beside him and up to the doorway. We stand and look into the room and the shock of seeing this six-year-old version of myself hits me in waves. Little Michael looks so vulnerable—the shaved head with the large white bandage taped askew across the incision scar, brown plastic horn-rimmed glasses framing his eyes. Beside him on the bed lie two books, *Charlotte's Web* and *We Love You, Snoopy*. He's holding another Peanuts book in his tiny hands.

The room has two other beds with small children in patterned pajamas in them, both sleeping. It's February, and for the first time I notice it's cold in here.

I look at myself, the six-year-old me, mere hours post-op, and I swallow hard. For some reason, it feels like I might get choked up if I allow it. I don't.

"Ready?" David asks.

"I think so. I don't know. I don't exactly know what to do. I don't know what to say."

"It's okay. It won't matter, because he won't remember any of it. *You* won't, that is. You know what I mean."

"Do I? All right. I'll just…I guess we'll talk to him."

"*You'll* talk to him. I'll be out here."

Now I look down, trying to make a stern face even though I feel more nervous. "Really? Seriously?"

"Seriously," he says. "It's fine. Just don't make it about you—about the grown-up version of you, I mean. Make it about him."

I nod and look back into the room. He is me. And I'm me. I feel afraid for him, knowing what he's going to have to endure in just a few short years—being bullied, abused, wanting to die. Starting to abuse alcohol, drugs. He's six now. A baby. And in another four years he'll be smoking. My God.

I pray: God, give me the strength to do this, whatever this is. Grant me the power to do what's required here, whatever that is.

Michael looks up when I enter the room, David standing alone in the hallway; presumably invisible to everyone but me. At this point, I don't even know.

"Hi," he says. *I* say.

He's me, I tell myself. *This is who I was at six.*

"Hiya, kid," I answer, not knowing what's going to come next. Will I mess this up, too? Try to warn him of something? Tell him I'm the grown-up version of him? No. I have to find the way to do this right, making it up as I go along.

He closes the cartoon book. "Are you a doctor?"

So he doesn't know me. There's no shock of recognition, of seeing himself in me. I have grown old—too old to recognize.

"No, I'm not a doctor. I'm…family." Already I feel I will stumble. I sit in the chair beside the bed, bracing myself against it. *Get hold of yourself.*

"Oh, okay," Michael says.

I can't help but think of him as Michael, not Mike. Like a parent using the child's proper name. I half expect him to ask more—who I am, my name. Something. But he's only six. He's thinking mainly of himself and his immediate family. *Make it about him.*

"Are my mom and dad coming back later?"

I clear my throat. "I'm not sure," I say. "I haven't seen them today."

"I had Jell-O," he tells me, and now I truly understand how young he is, how young I was when I was in this bed with a fractured skull. I wonder distractedly how long he's been out of the anesthesia. I'm glad I can't see the incision, or the indentation in the skull from the accident. It hurts my heart to think of it.

"Oh, you had Jell-O," I say, not knowing what else to say. I don't have children, and this version of me is a child—bright, to be sure, but not a child with a whole other secret life, like David.

"See my Peanuts books?" He shows off the copy of *We Love You, Snoopy* and another called *This Is Your Life, Charlie Brown.*

"Nice. Your parents get those for you?"

"Yup," he nods smartly. "My brother and I wrote to Charles M. Schulz and sent him some cartoons we drew. We said he could put them in his comic strip if he wanted. Mrs. Perry told me I shouldn't expect him to write back to us, but he did. He sent us a letter and some cartoons and a paper with Snoopy's paw print on it and everything."

"Really," I say. I remember this all so well. Surprising, considering how much I have forgotten about so much else. "And is Charles M. Schulz going to use your cartoons in Peanuts?"

"No," he says, shaking his head. The facial expression is so shockingly serious, I have to suppress a laugh. Damn, I really was a funny, expressive kid. "No, he said in his letter that he appreciated us sending the cartoons but that he couldn't use them, or it wouldn't be *his* comic strip anymore."

Amazing. That's exactly what the letter said, I remember.

"I think that's true. It was nice of you to send them, though. And it was nice of him to write back to you."

"Yes. He lives out in California where my Aunt Jane lives now. I'm hoping we can go out there to see her, and maybe meet Charles M. Schulz, too."

Like a punch in the gut, I flash back to that trip. Little Michael will fly for the first time to California about four years from now. Age ten. The whole family will go. Aunt Jane will be drunk when they arrive. There'll be an argument, and some of it will get ugly. I know all this not because I remember any of it. I blocked it somehow. I only know because my brother Bob will tell me the story, thirty, maybe forty years later. They'll pay a visit to the hockey rink Charles M. Schulz built, the Peanuts souvenir store. None of them will ever meet the man who created Snoopy and Charlie Brown.

All this blazes up and subsides in a moment while little Michael chatters away, oblivious to those gathering storm clouds. He's lucky to even be here, to survive the skull fracture more or less intact. He'll miss a total of fourteen days of school. He'll return to class by way of the short bus, riding with special needs children, terrified by an overly friendly one the size of an adult. He'll have to wear a batting helmet, and other kids will treat him differently for a long time. Rumors that he had to have a steel plate put in his head. Girls standing up for him when another boy picks on him. Shame, anger, degradation.

Age six.

And so my heart aches when I look down on the tiny figure on the bed with his cartoon books and his Jell-O. Is it feeling sorry for yourself if you're feeling sympathy for the child version of you, knowing not only the suffering that's taken place, but also the suffering to come?

He smiles up at me.

"That would be great if you got to meet Charles M. Schulz," I say. "That would be really cool."

TWENTY THREE

BOOM. Gone yet again. No chance to say whatever else I may have wished to say. Have I done enough? Did I do my job, whatever that was? I don't know. Too late to do anything about it now. Goodbye, little Michael. Goodbye, little me.

I'm back in the room again, or some facsimile of it. I suppose this is where I have to go to recover—to get over the feelings of sadness, frustration, grieving for the souls of Phil Ochs, Coleridge, Faulkner, my aunt…all of them.

Do I add myself to the list? Do I grieve my lost child-hood? Or do I envy little Michael the time he still has ahead of him, the good times as well as the bad? I don't know. So much to think about, but still I don't even know how I feel about what's happened only moments ago.

I stand up from the edge of the bed and walk to the painting beside the mirror on the wall. It's funny how every time I go from the adventure du jour—whether in merry Olde England or some afterlife realm of Kings of Coordinators—I inevitably return to something as mundane as a little hotel room with a pointillist-style painting on the wall. The names change, the faces change, even the room itself changes a bit, but it's all the same story.

Might as well examine the painting again. First I check myself in the small mirror beside it. I'm me again: in my fifties, modern glasses, dressed in normal street clothes. Nothing remarkable there. The painting? I don't know. Maybe a few more dots somewhere, but not much different from the way it looked before. It's a face…or will be, anyway, at some point. More and more, I get the distinct impression that it's important, but no idea how or why.

I'm alone in the room, but again I don't know if that will last, or whether I should head out the door. Meeting myself somehow changes the dynamic for me, but again I don't know how or why.

Where does it all lead? What does it mean? It's become harder and harder, not easier at all. When I've learned things in the past, lessons, skills, it seems to me that practice makes perfect to some degree. At worst, familiarity breeds contempt or boredom. But with this, I feel it getting closer to the bone as I progress through meeting Aunt Jane, my brother, myself as a boy. I feel a sense of pressure ratcheting up more and more.

I can't see any point in hanging around here longer than necessary, so I just go for the door right away. It opens onto a scene I never expected. Instead of a generic parking lot for a standard issue hotel, outside the door is a church. The room I'm leaving is within a school, as if it were a classroom. It makes no sense, but then, not much seems to make sense anymore. I haven't even shaken off the experience in the hospital, and now this.

Even more shocking, I'm instantly aware it's winter here and I'm dressed in a heavy coat, pants, gloves, and hat. I wasn't wearing them a moment ago—was I? I don't think so. The jarring effect of the view of the church and the school behind me almost makes me dizzy. I feel sick. I try to open the door again, retreat into the room, but it's locked.

I know the school, of course. I know the church. It's St. Joseph's, Bristol, Connecticut. I don't even have to guess the timeframe or reason: it's late 1977 or early 1978. This was my junior high. That church, St. Joseph's, has a small cemetery attached to it. I can see a few headstones from here. Another six or seven years from this time and my grandmother and grandfather will be buried here.

My breath comes in short bursts of steam as the wave of sadness and rage comes over me. I already know exactly why I'm here, although there's not a soul around. I'm going to see, and maybe try to somehow comfort, the thirteen-year-old version of myself.

Early adolescence can be the hardest, most turbulent time in life, and mine was no exception. It was incredibly painful because I made a simple error in judgment: after I discovered masturbation, I told another kid about it.

He took my confiding in him as some kind of sexual threat. He decided I must be gay to make such a confession.

And when he told all the other boys in the class, they believed him.

This is the time I'm revisiting now. I'm sure of it. Within the space of a few days, I go from a friendly, popular kid to an absolute pariah. Every boy in that class knows me as the masturbator—none of *them* do it, of course—and they're convinced I'm gay as well.

Denying it means it must be true. Denying it only makes things worse. I'm attacked in class, attacked on the blacktop basketball court.

I have to fight for my life.

When another of the building's metal doors flies open and boys pour out onto the cold blacktop in their white shirts and green pants and ties, I stand watching in silence. I'm not usually invisible in these visits to the past, but today I can't help thinking I must be. What purpose could it serve otherwise? I doubt I'm going to be the adult breaking up children fighting.

Sure enough, this is it—the day I'm attacked on the playground. Ironic word in this situation. There's no play here, and the ground is covered by this hard, icy blacktop beneath our feet. The boys spill out into a whirling dervish of malice. The shape of this mob is like that of an octopus, swarming and falling in on itself. I hear the words, words misapplied to me, and my outrage rises far beyond just for myself. It's for all the abused, all the broken, all the damned.

"Fucking faggot."

"You're a fucking pussy, man."

And then I see myself, the teenaged me, in the middle of that savage group of thirteen. The dreadful bowl haircut so popular to the time, and a look in my eyes that I can't describe as anything other than devastated.

"Leave me alone," I hear Michael say. "You guys are full of shit."

Not a single adult around, not even a nun. They have turned this little mob loose outside without a thought of supervision. This must be their only respite from them, a fifteen-minute recess where the little monsters can do as they like. The girls in our class are nowhere to be seen, and I suppose that meant they had a separate recess from us boys. I don't recall anything about it. So much my mind has blocked, mercifully.

The mob swirls around, and at length I see a boy hit me. My own adult body winces in sympathy pain. It was horrific enough to be that victim, surrounded by a group, in the full knowledge there wasn't a single friend among them. Yet watching it happen is somehow worse. The outrage in my heart makes the ringing in my ears jump from an eight to a ten.

Michael hits back, but without success. The kid is rangy, taller, longer arms. He's outmatched, like a boxer with a shorter reach. The mob is almost irrelevant, I can see, though I know it didn't feel that way.

I step forward, meaning to intervene if I can somehow. And in that moment, I feel a small hand up against my leg.

It's David, appearing to me for the first time in this brutal tableau, though I have no idea how long he's been here. He holds up the hand and shakes his head no. I see him mouth the words, *It's okay*.

It's not okay. But I understand now—I can't move. I'm frozen here, powerless to intervene. I can't change the course of history one iota. For once, I can't even talk to any of them.

My heart pounds as I look back to the awful scene before me. Like so many teenage fights, the mob is egging it on, but no one cheers for Michael. The kid hits him again, and then they tussle, an ugly flurry of hooded jackets and flying arms. I know what's coming, but when it happens, it's still a shock: the bully pulls Michael's hood, *my* hood, over my face. Blows rain down, blows unseen.

But now I see them as they happen. And I see what I couldn't have seen at the time: the ugly mob of jeering boys cheers the bully on as he fights dirtier. Fists pumping into the air.

"Yeah, get him. Fuck him up."

I watch the small body sag as little Michael surrenders. He falls, every last bit of fight bullied, beaten, out of him.

The crowd scatters. Back to normal. Who cares? Forget that kid.

At last, David's hand drops. I look at him and notice that he's translucent again.

And so am I.

David nods, and I understand somehow what I have to do. It's the only thing I can do.

I walk to the boy, the small, crumpled figure. His face is red—distorted with rage, shame, silent tears. I hold my translucent hand up and wipe the tears from his eyes. I wrap my arms around him in a hug that he can neither feel nor return.

Then I, too, begin to cry.

TWENTY FOUR

THIS TIME I BLINK ONCE AND AM BACK IN THE ROOM AGAIN AT THE EDGE OF THE BED, NO LONGER HUGGING A CHILD VERSION OF MYSELF BUT INSTEAD HOLDING MYSELF AS IF AGAINST THE CHILL WIND OUTSIDE THE CATHOLIC SCHOOL. David is right beside me, thankfully.

"That was intense. You okay?"

I let go, and my arms drop to my sides. "I'm okay. That one hurt. Did I really give him some kind of comfort? I sure don't remember feeling comforted by anyone or anything that day."

"You did," he says. "In that moment, you were a whizzer. Your soul cast a shadow that the teenage version of you felt. I know it probably doesn't seem like much."

I look at him, his wise eyes, so innocent yet somehow knowing. I can't help feeling protective, like he shouldn't have been there to witness a scene of such savagery.

I say as much. "Sorry you had to see that. You shouldn't have to see or hear things like that at your age."

"It's okay," he says. "I've seen worse."

"Seriously?"

"I know kids can be assholes."

I look at him with mild surprise, but in this moment the beating and curses he witnessed are so much graver than the fact that he knows a minor curse like *asshole*.

"What's happening? I feel like your innocence has been stolen somehow. I don't mean you existing in some weird afterlife we share, or meeting up with famous people from history. I mean you bearing witness to anything like today."

"Man's inhumanity to man," he says. "I know. It's awful."

"I never even heard those words you heard today until I was at least a few years older than you."

He comes forward, standing before me where I sit at the edge of the bed, and puts one tiny hand on my shoulder. He holds it there. "It's okay. Really. I don't like it, but it helps me understand we're all connected. They're a part of me I don't like, but they're still a part of me."

"What do you mean?"

David smiles. "We're all connected—you, me. Everyone. Even those kids."

"Ugh. That's a disgusting thought. I've thought it before, in kind of an abstract, philosophical way. But being connected to those little turds in any way makes me feel sick."

"I understand."

"I knew I couldn't resent them my entire life. I've been sober a long time. I prayed for them. I forgave them all a long time ago."

"Did you?"

I sigh, and feel my shoulders sag. "I prayed for them, anyway."

David laughs, and I chuckle a bit with him.

"And now you've forgiven them for real, at last," he says.

"How do you know?"

Before taking his small hand from my shoulder, he pats it a couple times—like a parent comforting a child.

"Because if you hadn't forgiven them just now, you wouldn't have cried."

I blink just once again, and when I open my eyes I'm in the passenger seat of a 1980s model American car, moving fast down the highway. I know this scene so well it amazes me. I tell the story often to other alcoholics, yet waking into it as an observer fills me with awe and dread. I always recall it as if it were a three-second video clip, a movie of my own life, yet I know this experience will last at least a little longer.

I'm twenty-three. I'm driving this car down Route Seventeen from Binghamton, New York, to my hometown in Connecticut. Even without looking over at the younger version of myself in this smoke-filled car, I'd know I have a cigarette in one hand and a bottle of Jack Daniels in the other. The tape deck in the car blasts Bob Dylan's *Tangled Up in Blue* at high volume, just as I remember it.

The boy is a young man now—survived junior high, survived high school, even survived college. Nearly finished with grad school. A quick calculation reminds me it's been ten years since the beating on the blacktop outside St. Joseph's. Ten years of smoking, drinking, drugs. Ten years of trying to kill the pain, with little success.

Flying down the highway, eighty miles an hour in the seventy zone, and somewhere in the middle of this song Dylan wrote when his marriage failed, another song's lyrics will drift through my head—or the title, anyway. It's a song most people only know as an instrumental, if they know it at all. It's the theme song from *M*A*S*H*, and the version I recall in these moments is the original song from the movie, not the TV series.

The name of the song: *Suicide Is Painless*.

I look over at myself, this younger version of me, who will think that thought at any minute. I wonder whether I'll see it somehow, a flicker in the eyes, like a candle guttering before the light goes out.

There. I see it. I see the pain flare up and fade, the eyes go back to a flatness they can only sometimes maintain.

I didn't remember crying during this drive, but after the thought of suicide, tears come next. Michael wipes them away angrily, pawing quickly with the hand that holds the cigarette in order to keep both hands mostly on the wheel. I look to the road ahead as we hit another patch of the infamous grooved pavement, the car hugging the highway around a precarious curve. He's looking for a bridge abutment, but there aren't any here.

He won't kill himself, of course. I'm living proof of that. There won't even be an attempt, a gesture, as it's called. At some point—maybe even on this drive—he'll think about it further.

He'll think, *If only I could find a big enough empty, abandoned building, I could get a can of gasoline, and some matches…*

No. The pain of the family left behind would make it unjustifiable. The only way to truly do it right would be to erase oneself, to disappear completely. But then they'd never know for sure, and that wouldn't be fair to them either. Goddamn it.

This is the bottom for me, although I won't know it for at least another year or so. This is what hitting bottom looked like.

How can I comfort him, me, this poor lost soul with his tenuous hold on life? We fly down the road at a furious speed, yet he's not aware he's hurtling toward a future. I can't intervene, of course, and besides, I'm not even here in a fully human form. I'm translucent, a ghost from the future, just as I was at the school from ten years earlier.

I reach my translucent left hand out and put it over his right hand, the one still tight around the bottle. I hold it there as the trees and bushes on Route Seventeen flash by, watching them go. I can't do anything else until I blink again into another world.

TWENTY FIVE

BACK IN THE ROOM AGAIN, FULLY ALERT, AWAKE. Apparently human and standing right in front of the painting with the tiny dots—so close, I can't even see it clearly. I realize I didn't even look at it last time, and barely looked at it the time before.

I step back, then back even more, look hard at it.

The face is clear now, though it's still a kind of pointillism. The features filled in so well, at last I can't help but know.

The face is my own.

I smile, and then I find myself suppressing a giggle. How did I not see it before? It all leads back to this, some kind of confrontation with the self, some kind of ego deflation.

There you are again. Let it go. The ego isn't you. It's something else.

It's all come full circle somehow, and in a way I can't explain, I already know my work with meeting famous people and close relatives and even earlier versions of me, is finished. And I thought I was alone here with this painting and this revelation, but I sense I'm not alone.

"Yes," says a small chorus of voices behind me.

When I turn, I'm not even surprised to see David, M'Extezuh, and the Coordinator standing behind me. They're lined up against the wall in a row like some beneficent trio of beings representing all the ages and worlds: youth and this world, the ancient and the great beyond, and something still mysterious and in-between.

"It's me," I say. "All this way I came, just to meet myself? Have I misread it?"

"Not at all," says the Coordinator. We stand, me facing them, but I feel somehow I am one of them now—not opposed, but joined together in some ineffable way. "There's a medical theory," he continues, "and it's somewhat supported by science, though the research is still bearing it out. All in good time, it will be proven, but at present it's still considered theoretical. This theory has to do with the sort of unpaid volunteer work you do, among your own kind, trying to help people gain or maintain recovery from alcohol, drugs, other addictions. There's some evidence that this work helps both people, regardless of motive or even belief in it."

"I think that's true," I say.

"Yes, but in all your years of experience, it's only been a feeling. Now science is at last catching up with the spiritual, demonstrating that there's an actual physiological benefit for both people in this equation. Think of it as being rather like endorphins, as when you pet a dog or cat, to break it down to its most basic form. When you pet the animal, the chemicals released in the brain provide a feeling of well-being to both the animal *and* you."

"So my next step is—what?"

"Helping complete strangers," he says without hesitation, and David and M'Extezuh nod in agreement. "Complete, non-famous strangers," he adds with a slight smile.

"And so now I'm a what? A player? A whizzer? I still don't think I understand all this, even now."

"A player is someone who has progressed through different levels of being a whizzer. First came the visits to famous people, which was all about ego gratification and awe. Then, in your case, close family relatives—still related to the ego, but more personal, less self-serving. Finally, one meets oneself; as you did, not once but three times.

"When one reaches the level of player, he or she becomes what you call *translucent*. You can still see yourself, as you did, but not appearing completely solid. You can, in effect, see through yourself. At that point, you can't speak to anyone, nor can they speak to you or even see you... unless, of course, they are another whizzer, as in the case when you saw David.

"Changing the past is not an option for you when you're a player. Only comfort. And you notice how naturally and without thought or effort you comforted your younger self."

I nod. "Yes."

The Coordinator moves back a step and as if on cue, David steps forward.

I look down at David without a word, and he says, "Remember what I told you a long time ago? When I go on my excursions, it's like I died. At that level, the souls of the dead don't have responsibilities. They get the chance to do good things. If they can do them, great. If not, that's okay. No one thinks about concepts like *failure* or *success*. Those are human concepts."

The Coordinator adds, "And once you attain that level, and have met yourself in some incarnation or other, then finally come strangers who are just regular people—help them with no thought of reward and you get a real reward, because it's essentially ego-less…or at least, it should be. Remember when you saw David in the children's hospital by that boy's bedside?"

"Yes, I remember."

"He didn't know him, never did. Never will. That is the highest level: giving comfort to a stranger with no thought of success or failure, no thought of reward."

"So now I've 'graduated,' what does that mean? That I'm at that level next?"

"Yours is to comfort the artist, the writer, the painter or poet," says the Coordinator. "And yes, you've done all you needed to do with those familiar to you, including family and even yourself. Now you'll return to your normal life for a time, but your future excursions will be with strangers—artists of some kind, to be sure, but not familiar to you. Not famous.

"You can go back and comfort them all you want, but in the end it's their art that redeems them…whether it's in the form of songs or paintings or poems, or even the lives themselves that they've led. Their art is at the heart of everything they'll ever know or have known, everything they'll ever be or have been."

I nod, saying nothing. There isn't anything to say. He's right.

And in that moment it occurs to me that M'Extezuh has been curiously silent all throughout this entire conversation. As if he reads my thought, his eyes light up, and he joins in, "This life—this temporary existence we're all in from day to day—is mostly an illusion. Just as in the song, *Merrily, merrily, merrily, merrily, life is but a dream*. And when you wake from this dream, you will know you are a perfect point of brilliant white light. In short, a soul. The body may die, but the soul never dies.

"You may not have known this before. Each soul, added to the next and the next, adds up to that totality we call *God*. A soul may be buried in pain for a lifetime, but it is still there. And in that soul, in every soul, lies the secret of all existence, the answer people spend a lifetime seeking. The answer, of course, is love. Remember that each day if you can."

A sudden chill seizes my spine, and he smiles.

"Look into the eyes of the person next to you and see the light," he says. "God is there. Look into the eyes of children, of conmen, of nurses and accountants, of beggars and saints, and see God is there. Then you will begin to know who you are, and you will know how to treat yourself, and others, too. As sacred.

"And now, go back to your wife. Go back to your life."

Another blink, and I'm in bed, huddled under the covers. Yes, I remember, all this has taken place while I was asleep.

I look at my wife, still sleeping. I know I can only aspire to be as good a person as her on any given day. I won't be better. But I also know everything that's happened was no dream. She sighs in her sleep and I lie back down beside her for a few moments more.

THANK YOU

I'm truly grateful to you for taking the time to read *Whizzers*. It is among the great accomplishments of my life.

If you'd like to check out my other novels, please visit my website at msahno.com. As a thank you for subscribing to my email newsletter, you'll get news on upcoming events, along with a free ebook, *Rides From Strangers.* This short story collection is only available to subscribers.

For today's independent authors, book reviews are like currency. If you enjoyed this novel, please post a review of it on Goodreads or Amazon. If you email me to let me know that you've reviewed it, I'll send you a special bonus PDF of exclusive material.

Of course, if you like the novel, I hope you'll recommend it to others and follow me on social media. You can find me on Twitter at twitter.com/MikeSahno and Facebook at facebook.com/sahnocomm.

Thank you all.
Mike

www.ingramcontent.com/pod-product-compliance
Lightning Source LLC
Chambersburg PA
CBHW030631190726

48286CB00008B/2486